Dear Lori —
 Please read. This is given with all my love —
  Mom.

That Very Special Person—
Me!

That Very Special Person—

Me!

Self-Esteem for Teens

Margaret Houk

HERALD PRESS
Scottdale, Pennsylvania
Waterloo, Ontario

Library of Congress Cataloging-in Publication Data
Houk, Margaret, 1932-
   That very special person—me! : self-esteem for teens / Margaret Houk.
     p. cm.
   ISBN 0-8361-3514-8
   1. Teenagers—Religious life. 2. Self-respect—Religious aspects—Christianity—Juvenile literature. 3. Teenagers—Conduct of life. 4. Self-respect—Juvenile literature. I. Title.
BV4531.2.H594 1990
248.8'3—dc20   89-29003
                                                                                 CIP

Verses marked TLB are taken from *The Living Bible* © 1971 owned by assignment by Illinois Regional Bank N.A. (as trustee). Used by permission of Tyndale House Publishers, Inc., Wheaton, Ill. 60189. All rights reserved.

THAT VERY SPECIAL PERSON—ME!
Copyright © 1990 by Margaret Houk. Published by Herald
   Press, Scottdale, Pa. 15683; released simultaneously in
   Canada by Herald Press, Waterloo, Ont. N2L 6H7. All
   rights reserved.
Library of Congress Catalog Card Number: 89-29003
International Standard Book Number: 0-8361-3514-8
Printed in the United States of America
Cover photo by Steve Skjold
Design by Jim Butti

97 96 95 94 93 92 91 90 10 9 8 7 6 5 4 3 2 1

CONTENTS

1. It's Good to Be in Love with Me 7
2. What Makes Me Special? 10
3. Who Am I? 15
4. I Want to Be Me 23
5. I Want to Feel Good About Myself 33
6. I Want to Look Good 42
7. I Need to Feel Good 50
8. I Want to Be Confident 59
9. I Want to Be Comfortable with My Feelings .. 70
10. I Want to Be a Good and Honorable Person .. 81
11. Getting Along with People 92
12. Resolving Conflicts 100
13. Building Friendships 107
14. My Sexual Self 114
15. Handling Hard Times 123
16. Looking Ahead 131

Looking at Me 134
My Listeners 136
The Author 137

*To him for whom
I live each day*

1.

It's Good to Be in Love with Me

One of our country's brightest stars in the mid-80s was Mary Lou Retton, teenaged Olympic gold medalist. More than just a superb gymnast, Mary Lou stood out from the crowd because she glowed with a special kind of warmth and charm—one that made everyone around her feel good. She smiled frequently, and laughed often. Mary Lou radiated an easily observable love for herself and what she was doing.

President Reagan won the hearts of his countrymen with the same cheerful qualities. Many who disagreed with his policies supported him nonetheless because of the person he was. He exuded confidence and was not easily shaken by fierce political attacks.

Both of these people had a large measure of

something called self-esteem. It can also be described as self-respect, a good self-image, or a sense of worth. It means feeling good about yourself, at the deepest level.

Self-esteem is essential for bringing out the best in you. It requires knowing yourself and liking what you are. Can you perform well on a test if you are nervous because you don't know or like the material? The same is true of your personal life. In order to do the best job of living, you have to be comfortable with yourself.

Self-esteem is vital to your loving people in a healthy way. Psychologists tell us you have to love yourself first before you can love others unselfishly. True love requires putting yourself out for someone without counting on getting anything back. Like when you help your sister with the dishes, even though it isn't your turn, just because she's tired.

Self-esteem tends to make a person more popular, because people are more comfortable around those who like themselves. Think for a moment about one or two persons you know who think well of themselves. Isn't it fun to be around them?

Self-esteem enables people to stand strong in the face of trials. Unjust criticism, meanness, and even your own goofs are easier to take when you know your strengths and weaknesses. You can then decide whether you really have a problem or not.

Self-esteem is not something you can buy or earn. You won't find it in a store, nor can anybody else give it to you. You have to give it to yourself.

You do this by healthy thinking and living. By developing the right attitudes about yourself. By making sound moral choices. By seeing yourself as God sees you—as his good creation, a beloved child, with something important to contribute to the world.

If God so grants, you will have a long journey ahead in life. You may as well make it an enjoyable one. That means preparing the way well. Building on the strong foundation of healthy self-esteem will make it better.

Not everybody can be a Mary Lou Retton or a Reagan. You may never be the football captain or homecoming queen. But even if you don't make first chair in band or become an eagle scout, you can still learn to be a confident, self-assured person—one who values himself or herself.

Self-esteem, however, is like a coat. It's not yours until *you* buy it, and it won't do you any good unless you put it on. This book will show you how.

2.

What Makes Me Special?

A child of the early 1900s, Agnes Bejaxhiu sat at her school desk in Skopje, Yugoslavia, listening to her teacher read letters from a missionary about his work in a Bengalese Indian mission. She was captivated. Volunteering her services at the age of eighteen, she served her Lord by teaching in a high school in Calcutta for twenty years.

But something was missing. One day, praying intently while riding a train, she received a "call within a call"—to devote the whole of her being to serving the needs of the outcasts of Asia. The more she tried to live like and for Christ, the more she came to believe that the real presence of Jesus was in every one of them.

You Are Unique

Agnes is better known as the beloved Nobel peace prize winner, Mother Teresa. She would say that you, too, are very special. That is because you are unique. There is only one *you.* No one else in history has ever been quite like you, and no one ever will.

Your mom and dad were raised differently from you, and also from each other. They don't always agree with each other, and they don't always agree with you. Neither do your friends. That's because nobody has looked at life through the same two eyes as you have for twenty-four hours a day the past umpteen years.

You are a combination of abilities, experiences, and values unlike that of anybody else. Nobody else looks and acts just like you.

Even identical twins have differing personalities. You don't believe that? Ask their parents. Or ask each of them a thought question sometime when they are not together. Something like, How will our country be able to keep the peace? You'll get two different answers.

Your particular ideas, interests, and skills don't come together in the same way as anyone else's. Nobody has done exactly the same things you have, in exactly the same way. Nobody else has quite the same thoughts, hopes, dreams, and loves as you do. That makes you unique, one of a kind.

You Are Precious

Because you are one of a kind, you are precious. We human beings have always valued uniqueness. You are irreplaceable. That means that no amount of money could ever give the world what you have to offer. You have a value beyond measuring.

You are also precious because you were created by God. You are priceless in his eyes. Genesis says that everything God made is "good." After he created the first person he looked around and saw that everything he had made was "*very* good."

You are precious because you are a human being. God took special pains when he made people. Unlike the animals which he simply called into being, he formed Adam from the earth and Eve from Adam's rib. Then he breathed into their nostrils to give them life.

Why do you suppose he went to so much trouble? Because he had a special feeling for people. We are created in God's image, meaning we have the ability to think, value, and appreciate what he has made, just as he did at creation.

We are "the crown of his creation," the best of his workmanship. You will someday learn in science classes, if you haven't already, that human beings are far superior in their development over any species in the plant or animal world.

You are precious because other people value you. Have you ever noticed how sad people are when they hear about someone getting hurt or killed? Often they don't even know these persons. Yet they value them, because human beings are precious to many others.

You are precious because you have the ability to love. Some people believe that God is present in every human being because of our capacity to love. Whether that is true or not, people are at their loveliest when they are showing love to others.

You are capable of that, too. Just for fun, write down or mentally count how many people you truly care about—family, neighbors, friends, teachers. Quite a sizable list, isn't it?

You Are Important

The characteristics that make you different also make you important. Because nobody else looks at life quite the same way you do, you have something new and fresh to offer the world—your particular way of looking at life and things. We call that your viewpoint or insight. No one sees with your eyes, or draws the same conclusions that you do.

Somebody somewhere needs your unique viewpoint. That makes you important. We human beings are better off when we benefit from the added input others can give us. Have you ever had a friend come up with a good idea for something fun to do, one that you hadn't thought of? In this way people expand each other's horizons.

You are important because God wants you, *you personally*, to be a part of his family in time and eternity. Yes, even though you sometimes let him down. Jesus came to earth to overcome sin and bring people into his heavenly Father's family forever. You are one of those for whom he came.

You Are Needed

You are part of a social system, your family. Each member of a family depends on one another for part of his or her happiness. Your family depends on you for that special something you have to offer them.

Have you ever had a pet cat or dog that died? The hurt is even worse if a member of the family dies. Nobody else can take that person's place or fill the emptiness.

You are likewise needed for your special place in your family. Even if your family has been split by divorce, you are needed for your particular contribution to both families.

In the same kind of way, your friends are also a *system.* They depend on you and you depend on them. You contribute something that is especially dear to each friendship that you have. If one of your buddies moves away, can the new kid on the block take his place? Of course not. You have the same kind of impact on your friends.

You are needed because no one can replace you. When that buddy moves away, the group can get along without him. The new neighbor might become a treasured friend. He might even contribute something important to the group. But the group will never again be quite the same as it was before your buddy left.

You Are Needed by God

All of the world's religions look for a meaning to life. The Christian faith says that God has a part or role for you to play in the drama that is life. David said, "You [God] saw me before I was born and scheduled each day of my life before I began to breathe" (Psalm 139:16, TLB). Jeremiah and the apostle Paul also claimed that God's plan for their lives was made before they were born.

He has a job for you, too. There was a reason you were born. There is a purpose for your being here. Sometimes we humans see it clearly, and sometimes we don't. But God does not do anything without cause, and he created you.

Your job is to find your destiny. It involves coming to know yourself and then developing the talents and interests which he gave you. The next chapter will help you along that road.

3.

Who Am I?

A woman named Sybil was sixteen different people. Varying in age from infancy to adulthood, two of them were male, the rest female.

Impossible? No, Sybil was a real person, the subject of a 1973 book which exposed the mind-boggling ways by which the battered child of a mentally sick mother and father tried to cope with life by assuming multiple personalities. Fortunately, after eleven years of therapy, her analyst helped her find her one true self.

* * *

Now that you are about to enter the world of adulthood, you are focusing more and more on who and what *you* are. It's tough to figure this out. The person I am is usually the person I know least well. Have you ever blurted something out in haste and then thought afterward, Why did I say that? Or done something unexpected and then said, Why did I do that? Often we don't know where our ideas or actions come from.

Where Did I Come From?

We humans gain our identity partly from our heritage. People gather confidence from seeing their ancestors as persons of dignity and worth. African American author Alex Haley in his best-selling book, *Roots,* disclosed a tribal ancestry he could be proud of. Adopted persons often anguish over their lack of knowledge about their birth families.

Family trees are captivating. They give you a sense of belonging to something bigger than yourself. It's fun to see whose eyes you inherited. Or to know you descended from a hero of pioneer days, or from a famous leader or official.

However, in every family tree there's usually a crooked branch somewhere. It's not so nice to discover that great-grandpa went to prison for bank robbery. Or that great-aunt Sally was a bar dancer and prostitute.

Even though you may find them fascinating, you are not responsible for either the glories of your noble ancestors or the inadequacies of the scoundrels. You may have inherited grandpa's red hair, but you didn't inherit his bad temper. Nor is great-uncle Harry's making the Olympic team to your credit.

Your heritage is fun, interesting, and a part of you. But it is not a valid measure of worth. Nor does it tell a lot about you personally.

Finding Me in My Family

The kind of family situation you grew up in has a major bearing on what you are. Most of your values come from your parents. If they believe education is important, so will you. If they are music lovers, your exposure to a variety of musical experiences will be great. If they like gourmet food, your taste buds will get a good programming. If God is number one in their lives, he most likely will rate very high in yours, too.

We pick up the habits and mannerisms of our parents. If Dad likes giving orders, his son is apt to do so. If Mom gets her way by behind-the-scenes plotting and planning, her daughter will probably do likewise.

Yet as we grow up, we can weigh the available models and choose our own style. If youths are turned off by their parents' actions, they may try hard to be just the opposite. The son may see his father as *bossy* and decide he would rather talk things over with people. The daughter may prefer to be straightforward with people. An adult friend may provide a good example to follow.

Where and how your family lives also flavors your personality. Farm people look at life differently than do city people. The lifestyle of New Yorkers varies from that of Southerners, Midwesterners, Texans, or Californians. Some families entertain their guests with linen dinner napkins, candlelight, and steak. Others prefer hot dogs cooked on the backyard grill.

Special family needs also color your perspective. Many youths today live in single-parent families. Divorce and remarriage often bring stepparent problems. If your elderly grandmother, stepsisters, or stepbrothers live with you, they give your everyday existence added depth and challenge. So does having a mentally retarded sister, or a serious illness within your family. Drug or alcohol addiction in a family member brings a costly, painful burden.

Your family's financial status affects how you look at life. Some families fly coast-to-coast on vacation or to visit other family members. Others have to plan ahead for travel trips and must go by car. Some cannot afford vacations away from home.

Finding Me in My Friends and Surroundings

Your neighborhood and school friends also have a bearing on what you are. Sarah was a vivacious, fun-loving teenager who yearned for more freedom. When she started walking to school with a new neighbor, Diane, she became moody. She started talking back to her parents and arguing with them frequently. When Sarah's parents broke up the friendship, the arguments slacked off. Sarah became more content. Obviously Diane had had a disturbing influence on Sarah.

Friends also influence you for the better. A group in my high school had ideals I admired. They welcomed the only African American female student in our grade into their midst. They nominated dependable students for class officers and came up with workable ideas on how to make our school better.

One day I told one of them about an idea for a class project. She liked the idea. Soon after, she invited me to a party. Several months later I had a cluster of new friends. When two of them became senior class officers, they asked me to serve on the executive committee, where I learned valuable organizing skills.

The learning process, too, helps us define who and what we are. We relate to some teachers better than others. Certain subjects come easier than others. The social and natural sciences give us a broader view of life. Classes in art, music, and drama add depth, variety, and richness to our lives.

Participating in sports, cheerleading, and the debate team provide opportunities to form friendships and build pride in a job well done. Programs like campfire girls, scouts, and 4-H help us find and develop extra skills and interests. They also help us uncover weaknesses and weed out some of our dislikes.

TV, Movies, Magazines, and Books

A wise person once said, "You are what you think about, all day long." Like it or not, many of our ideas about ourselves and life come from the impact of television or movies on our thinking. Song lyrics also sway us, as do the books and magazines we read. They give us subtle messages and shape our attitudes.

Often they send erroneous messages, such as, Every problem can be solved, or, No one will love you if your ears stick out. They also send dangerous ones, like, You can't have fun without alcohol or adventurous thrills.

A favorite false theme is that life is not worth living without your one and only true love. Untrue. Every day someone loses a sweetheart and still sees purpose in going on. Often persons in that situation find deep, heartfelt love again. In a later chapter, you'll see more examples of these subtle messages and learn how to screen what you're seeing or hearing.

Newscasts also impact on us while showing us what's going on in the world. Reports of the African famine brought about one of the greatest humanitarian efforts in history to relieve the suffering of a starving people.

Rock Music and Other Teen Statements

Part of you comes from the era in which you live. Every generation of teenagers comes up with its own set of ideas, behaviors, and music to declare its independence.

This is both good and bad. It is good because society needs fresh, creative answers for the problems it has not been able to solve. By saying, We will do it differently, each new generation unites and solidifies its determination to find new ways.

It becomes bad if the teen statement is destructive. Pro-suicide rock lyrics exist. "Drugs are great!" and "Sex is the ultimate high" are two statements that for several years caused many teenagers untold grief, and in a few cases their lives. As you grow in your teen years, you will need to recognize what is dangerous in the statement of your peers and to make your own decisions accordingly.

Sometimes the teen statement is problematic. That is, it is neither good nor bad but apt to cause problems for you. For instance, it might cause trouble between you and your parents. We will talk about solving these kinds of problems in a later chapter.

My Spiritual Grounding Matters

Your church life and the religious teachings you've had also play a role in what you are. If your family has enjoyed a rich spiritual life and you have spent many years learning God's will, you will tend to feel close to God and his church. You will most likely see yourself as God's obedient servant.

Church teachings—the creeds, confessions of faith, catechism, Scripture, hymns, and prayers—have a way of sticking with us. In 1980, Iranian hostage Kathryn Koob kept her faith alive during the 444 days she was held captive by relying on spiritual teachings she had learned while young. Prisoners of war, victims of terrible accidents and natural catastrophes, and persons in other terrorizing situations put substance to their faith by remembering and repeating familiar psalms, Bible verses, prayers, and hymns.

Church teachings also keep us on track. Karen's mom was taking mood-altering pills. When she got into her teens, Karen started taking them, too. It was just "mild stuff," Karen told herself. Harmless.

Then one day Karen's mom needed money to buy more. She talked Karen into burglarizing a nearby house. Karen did, and got caught.

"I want to obey the commandment to honor my mother, but how can I when my mom does this to me?" she asked. But Karen also knew the Seventh Commandment, telling her not to steal. She knew that God's will comes before people's. Eventually she admitted she knew better and had to be held accountable for her wrongdoing.

Surprisingly, church teachings can have a negative effect. Many teenagers magnify their mistakes. They condemn themselves because they are sinners, and God hates sin. They tend to overlook the importance of the fact that Jesus came to take care of that problem once and for all. He wants us to regret our sins, confess them, and make amends.

Then we need to trust in God's forgiveness, put the failings behind us, and get on with our lives.

Are you able to forgive yourself for yesterday's goofs? Or do you keep on rehashing your mistakes? Which way expresses God's kind of love better?

Finding Me in Myself

All of the above are outside influences in your life that help to determine who and what you are. But you are more than part of a heritage, a family, your school and church, your friends, and your surroundings. A big part of you, perhaps the biggest, is what you are in and of yourself. The next chapter will help you find *you* in yourself.

4.

I Want to Be Me

Bill wanted to be a teacher. He loved kids and he loved learning. But he came from a family of preachers, and his folks wanted him to follow in their footsteps. So he tried.

He went through prep school and entered the seminary. He got through several courses but simply couldn't master Hebrew and Greek. Eventually he washed out and ended up—you guessed it—a teacher.

"Let each bird sing its own song." Is this how *you* feel? Do *you* want to sing *your* own song? Do you sometimes find yourself saying, I want to be *me*?

Great! You need to feel that way. You will live a happier life if you are true to your inmost needs and wants. It's healthier for you.

It's also important that you do. As we see in Bill's story, everybody has to find his own place in the world. God gave us certain equipment. We do the best job for God when we discover ours and run with it.

It's good that nobody has quite the same equipment. We are all the more interesting as people because we are different. Wouldn't it be a boring world if we were all alike? All salespersons, or truck drivers? All soccer players, or needlecrafters?

Who Am I, Really?

Someone has said, "You are not who you think you are, you are not who others think you are, but you are who *you think* others think you are." What do you think that means?

We all want to be accepted by others. We want them to like us. Or at least to respect us. We ask, Do I look all right? Or say, I can't get up in front of a bunch of people. I'm too shy. Or, I couldn't do that! What would people think?

The way in which others see us has great impact on our lives, so we try to imagine what they see. Often we imagine wrong. We exaggerate and condemn any little thing that is unusual or that we don't like about ourselves. Like a nose that is a bit longer than normal. Or red hair. Or freckles. A loud laugh. A deep voice. Or a few extra pounds.

The funny thing is, other people don't dislike those things about us. They don't even *notice* them nearly as much as we do. They are too busy worrying about themselves.

It pays to be aware of what others think, but it's also important to see yourself as you really are.

I Am My Own Person

In the last chapter, we saw that you are part of

your family, church, school, and surroundings. You are at the same time your own person. That person is hard to pin down because what you are depends a lot on the people you are with and what you are doing at any given time.

Fifteen-year-old Steve is cool and smooth around girls, but around his dad he gets nervous and fidgety. With his mom he cooks often, is relaxed, and laughs a lot. In front of the class at school he looks down, avoids questions, and shifts his weight from one foot to another. When he plays his saxophone in the jazz band he's in total control, his head in another world.

You, too, are many things to many people. You are different things at different times. It's not easy to find yourself. You need to know what to look for and how to go about it.

I Am a Body

The first thing you are is a physical body with a certain appearance. You are either short, or medium height, or tall. You are heavyset, middleweight, or slender. Your eyes, skin, and hair have a particular color. The hair is either straight, curly and thick, or thin. Some noses are straight, some turn up, and some curve down. Together, your facial features and body form make up your personal appearance. Your appearance is the entrance gate to opportunities in your life. By one's appearance people learn whether a person is neat, careless, sophisticated, sharp, or carefree.

We want lots of friends. We want to be generally respected. We want to be able to get the job we apply for. So we try to present ourselves well.

The way your appearance comes across to other

people is called a *first impression*. We try particularly hard to make a good first impression, because often much depends upon that. If you are applying for a job, a well-groomed appearance tells a future employer that you will be careful with his goods. A neat, clean image may impress that new boy or girl in school whom you want to meet. Presenting a good appearance at church and school indicates that you respect those institutions. It thus draws respect from the people who gather there.

How you present yourself also makes a difference in the friends you make. Youths find they are usually most comfortable around persons of similar income. It's no fun chumming with people who go sailing a lot if your idea of a good afternoon is limited to baseball at a local park.

First impressions can be wrong, as when a usually punctual person has a flat tire and arrives late for a job interview. Though often hard to erase, wrong impressions can be set straight later. And, no matter what first impression you make, people will soon move on and begin to see you as a total person.

My Interests Identify Me

First impressions are just that. Shortly after you open your mouth, people begin turning their attention away from how you appear and start noticing other things. Your interests and abilities begin to show. When Brian carries on about how good the football team is this year, you know he's into sports. When he spouts off dozens of statistics about the top pros in the National Football League, you know he has the memory of an elephant.

It's interests that carry us past first impressions.

If Dave, talking to Brian, doesn't give a hoot for athletics, he'll try to change the subject. If the two can't find an interest in common, one of them will soon say, See ya later, and hope it doesn't happen. If, however, they pursue the conversation a bit farther and discover they both love working on cars, a friendship may be in the making.

Our interests usually (but not always) lie in those areas where we have skills and talents.

My Talents Are Gifts from God

The world needs a diversity of talents. So does God. He compares church people to parts of a body, all of which are important to its functioning full and well. In fact, God gives greater importance to "the lesser parts." God's greatest work is done by many little people, doing little things.

There is a story about a house badly in need of paint. The paint can said, "I can do the job." But the brush thought it was more important. The ladder said, "What could you do without me?"

"You couldn't get anywhere without me," said the checkbook. The painter himself was standing back, laughing.

Do you know where your talents are? It takes time to discover all of one's potential. You need to try lots of things. With some of them you will fall flat on your face. But that's part of discovering what you are and are not capable of.

Do you think of yourself as *dumb*? Everybody is, in some area or other. Don't just look at the areas where you fall down.

What can you do as well or better than the average person? Haven't found it yet? Keep trying. Leslie Lemke was a blind, retarded cerebral-palsied child who never learned to walk or talk normally. Yet he unleashed fabulous abilities on the piano suddenly one night around the age of twenty. He can play anything he hears, after having once heard someone else play it. He also sings whatever he's heard once, with a voice that can still not quite pronounce all English vocal sounds.

Do you feel *dumb* in school because you can't get top grades, no matter how hard you try? Your abilities may lie in another field. Society has trouble recognizing adequately all kinds of abilities. Not everybody has a high level of *school-type* skills. Not everyone is college material. Where would society be without plumbers and auto mechanics? Typists and truck drivers?

Scrubbing floors and running cash registers also fulfills God's purposes and human needs in life. Every person uses the basic tools of communication learned in school, but beyond that, how well you develop your talents is what counts. In the Bible, Mary was criticized by one of the disciples for anointing the feet of Jesus with costly ointment. Jesus defended her because she was doing what she could do for her Lord, out of love.

After interests and abilities, personality and character begin to play a big role in telling people what you are. Even if they both like fixing cars, Dave and Brian won't become friends if they rub each other the wrong way. If Dave likes to clown around and Brian doesn't, they may not hit it off. If Brian "borrows" tools and never returns them, Dave may not want to hang around with him.

Looking at Personality and Attitudes
Your personality is your way of talking, acting,

and behaving. It is your combined thoughts and feelings and how you act upon them. Do you want to be *you* on the inside as well as the outside? Good! God wants that for you, and so do the people who care about you.

Are you a natural clown, or a quiet scholar? A brain, or a slow and deliberate thinker? A crier, or a laugher? A fighter, or one who backs off from a conflict? Are you naturally neat, or more comfortable with a certain amount of ordered confusion? Whatever your answers, you are what you are, and that's okay.

There is no right or wrong to personality. The world needs all kinds of people, for balance. Tough people need gentle people and the gentle need aggressive friends. Quiet people need assertive people, and the assertive need relaxed, easygoing companions. Neatnicks need occasional disorder, and disorganized people need neatness once in a while.

It's not your personality but what you do with it that can get you into trouble. Take fighting, for example. If you were battling for your life from a bad auto accident, everybody would be glad you were a fighter. But if you punched some other guy out because he looked at you cross-eyed, your fighting nature would be causing you to disturb the peace and lose rather than make friends of others.

Closely related to personality is attitude. Attitudes are the mental positions people take about things. A friend of mine says every morning, "It's a beautiful day." Whether it's sunny or raining, hot and humid, or 20 degrees below zero, for him it's a beautiful day.

Needless to say, he is an enjoyable person to be

around. Attitudes spread. If you are around a grouch, you soon feel grouchy. If you are surrounded by cheerful persons, you feel cheerful.

Looking at Character and Values

If personality reveals how a person is, *character* reveals what that person stands for. Character is particularly important. Who wants to hang around with a locker thief or a gossip? Their friendships only last as long as it takes a person to figure out that he or she could be their next victim.

Character is based on values. Your *values* are your rating scale. Is this assignment important, or not? Is talking back to Mom or Dad good, or bad? Is this sweater worth more to me, or is that one? Our values include our likes and dislikes and also our sense of right and wrong.

Likes and dislikes don't often get us into trouble. Sooner or later most people come to respect the differing tastes of others. But moral decisions are a bit harder to handle. We need God's help and the counsel of God's people to know right from wrong.

God gave you a *free will,* that is, the right to make choices. But this carries with it a responsibility—to choose well. Sometimes it's hard to make those choices. You get confused about what is right or wrong. So another part of being *you* is deciding what your moral values will be. We will discuss this in more detail in a later chapter.

My Spiritual Self

There is a dreamer within you that moves you along life's road. What are your hopes and plans for your life? Do you want marriage? A family? Singleness? Adventure? Travel? Lots of learning?

How ambitious are you? Do you want to go to college? Do you want to be a doctor, or a teacher? Do you want full-time work for God?

What goals have you set for yourself? First team football? A part in the school play? Eagle Scout? Summer camp counselor?

These, too, are a vital part of you.

Is This Me, or Somebody Else?

We've discussed the outside and inner forces that work together to make you uniquely *you.* But few teens are comfortable with what they are. They don't like their hair. Or they feel awkward about the way they gesture. So they try imitating other people they see and like. When Michael Jackson and Madonna first became stars, teenagers all across the country tried to dress and act like them.

Teens also often feel a need to do the *in* thing. For one group that means designer jeans. For another, stone-washed jeans. For yet another, the punk look.

Imitating others and following trends are prompted by the desire to be accepted. There is nothing wrong with conforming, if you are being true to God, yourself, and your values. But if you don't like what is happening or don't believe what is being said, you won't be happy with yourself if you go along with the crowd.

What you are looking for is to feel good about yourself. What you need is to find your own style. That will come, in time. You can't hurry it. You have to feel your way along, even experiment a bit, until you piece together a lifestyle that fits you.

In the process, it's good to stay within limits that are God-pleasing. You can't feel good about yourself if your conscience is pricking.

You'll make mistakes, but you'll learn from them. If you pray for guidance, open yourself to wisdom from God's people, and listen to your heart and conscience, you'll make fewer goofs. You can also learn by copying the ways of older teens and other persons whom you like and respect.

5.

I Want to Feel Good About Myself

While on a choir tour, I was warned not to drink too much water between stops. I paid no attention. One afternoon while riding the bus, I got the urge to *go*. No way could I make it to our destination, an hour away. I had to ask the bus driver to stop at the next gas station.

The lead tour bus, traveling ahead of us, wondered why our bus wasn't following. It turned around and came back to check. Everybody knew! Upon arriving at our destination, the choir director grinned and said to me, "My, this is your day, isn't it?" My face was as red as an apple.

* * *

As a teen, there was nothing I wanted more than

to be all grown up. It would be so neat, not to make any more embarrassing blunders. Toward the end of my teens, I thought I had it made. No more goofs, I figured. I figured wrong. They didn't stop.

I didn't really grow up until I learned we never stop making mistakes. As we grow older, we make them less often. We also learn how to handle them better. We develop this poise by coming to know and accept ourselves and life better.

The Road Ahead

Your teenage years are the years to find yourself. To get comfortable with your body, mind, and abilities. To explore all the parts of your personality—your likes, dislikes, moods, habits—to find what you are comfortable with. To examine the moral values you've inherited and decide which ones work well and which don't, which ones you want and which you don't want. By the end of your teens the inside of you (what you think you want to be) and the outside (what you actually are) should be starting to come together.

In the meantime, it's a hard time for you. Adolescence is a challenge. Teenagers react in varying ways and degrees. Some can't stand their acne, but willingly observe curfew. Others want more say on freedom to come and go, but their appearance doesn't bother them as much. What works for a friend may not work for you. Each person has to find his or her own way.

It's not enough to know you are God's special creation, put on this earth for a reason. Nor can you find worth solely in your family, surroundings, and your own inner person. In an imperfect world where God's purposes and people's well-being are often hidden, distorted, or perverted, coming to believe in yourself takes effort. Self-esteem is something you have to work at.

You can start by taking a look at what you have to work with.

Looking at Me

How would you like to take an *outside* look at yourself, to see what others are seeing? You'll probably be surprised at what you find. Most people like themselves a lot better than they think they will.

You can have that view by turning to the back of this book and filling out the form called *Looking at Me*. I've put it at the end so you can quickly and easily come back to it and see yourself often in the next few years. It helps, when you get down on yourself, to take a look at the fine person that you truly are.

When filling out the form, leave blank the last line in each section, titled *Loving Me*. You will be filling that in later.

If you have trouble deciding upon the correct answers, ask members of your family or friends for their help. Most of the time others see us better than we do.

Good Messages

You build self-esteem by getting in the habit of giving yourself good messages. You need to look at what you are and say, That person is okay. It's even better to say, That person is interesting. The best message is, I really like the person that I am.

It isn't enough to say these things. You have to come to believe them. Insincerity shows. A friend of mine says frequently, "Hey, I'm the greatest, man!" Then he looks around to see what response he's getting. He himself isn't convinced. People who believe themselves capable of excellence don't need to brag about it.

You build self-esteem by recognizing that much of what you experience as a teenager is normal for your sex, generation, and age. It's comforting to know that you're not alone. Lots of teenagers feel self-conscious and get embarrassed easily. Many of the teenagers around you are just as nervous as you are around the opposite sex.

Something else you need to be aware of is that teenagers tend to be hard on themselves, yet kind to others who have the same kinds of problems. It's understandable if your best friend slips on ice and skins a shin, right? Then you don't need to think it so bad if it happens to you.

If you talk to yourself as you would to your best friend under similar circumstances, you'll find it easier to give yourself good messages. As you gain self-esteem, you are, in effect, becoming your own best friend.

Loving Me

Now please leaf to the back of the book, find the form entitled *Looking at Me*, and do the following:

- Look again at *physical characteristics*. Then ask yourself, What don't I like about my appearance? Have I ever found that objectionable in someone else? If not, on the line titled *Loving Me*, write "This person looks okay (or good, or fine, or attractive) to me," whichever is most true.

- Look at *skills, talents, and interests*. Then ask, Would I have fun with someone who does these things? If so, write on the bottom line in this section, "This person looks like lots of fun" (or interesting, or exciting, or fascinating, or however you feel about the possibilities you see there).

• Look at *personality traits*. Remember, there is no right or wrong about personality characteristics. Then ask, Would I like a friend with these qualities? Write on the last line, "This person has an interesting (or appealing, or charming, or lovable) personality."

• Look at *character traits*. Then ask, Does this person have "good" character? Does he or she try to please God and other people? If so, write on the bottom line, "This is a fine person, a credit and an honor to (his/her) parents and God."

• Look at *hopes, dreams, and goals*. Then ask, Is this the kind of person I would enjoy spending my time with? If so, write on the last line, "This person is enjoyable. I really like (him/her)."

Now reread your bottom lines. Isn't it a nice feeling to be a good friend to yourself?

Recognizing Poor and Incorrect Messages

In this imperfect world not all messages you pick up from your peers, others around you, and society are good messages. To build self-esteem you need to recognize which messages are untrue, or not good for you. You need to be *in the know*, to see life, people, and public attitudes for what they really are. As was mentioned earlier, you can't feel good about yourself if you run into trouble because you are misinformed.

We read in an earlier chapter that a lot of what we absorb from television, books, movies, magazines, and music lyrics is not true. And it is not accepted by society nor healthy for relationships. We tend to make heroes of the characters we see, hear, and read about. But today's media heroes often have faults that we ought not copy. Millions of fans loved Dr. Benjamin "Hawkeye" Pierce on the television show, *M.A.S.H.*, for his compassion and his crusading against war. But in the early episodes he frequently broke military rules and played around sexually with women.

Persons who don't respect rules are hard to live and work with. Most women don't like their bodies used as tools for somebody's lust. *M.A.S.H.* in its later years had to play down Hawkeye's unruliness and womanizing.

Bill Cosby's family comedy brought to television good workable ideas on how to solve problems, but few parents have Dr. Cosby's training in psychology or the time to be as understanding as he appeared to have on the show. Undoubtedly, he has had times in his own personal life when he was unable to meet his children's needs, and problems he was unable to solve. That's the way life is.

Soap operas are fascinating to watch, but in real life most lovers aren't that romantic. Also, people have jobs and just can't take off on a moment's notice to be there for each other, as the soaps so often portray.

There has been a trend in recent years toward more open, freer sexual relationships between people, particularly outside of marriage. Television drama and soap writers have exaggerated this trend because they like to see themselves as being on the forefront of change. Their characters engage in sexual activity in almost every romantic scene.

Statistics on public attitudes show that many

people have not accepted this immoral style of living. God's laws are written for the good of all human beings. Free and open sex does not work well for people. The trend is beginning to reverse.

Newscasts also need to be viewed with an open mind. The news media's first concern is to create an interesting story, even if there isn't one on a particular day. For this reason reporters will blow all out of proportion such insignificant events as our nation's president slipping and falling down. News stories also sometimes paint unrealistic pictures of how bad things really are in the world, for dramatic effect.

Advertising can also distort how things really are. Advertising carries subtle messages that encourage us to buy. For instance, cosmetics advertisers suggest that the use of their product will bring romance into our lives. There's nothing *that* magic in cosmetics. Car ads promise big thrills, and having that first car does mean a lot. But for most people cars are just handy tools to get us somewhere.

Advertising models and the romantic leads in movies and television suggest height, weight, and other personal appearance standards that are not typical of Miss Jane or Mister John Q. Public. The famous much-loved Norman Rockwell paintings display people more accurately.

Finding the Truth

It's important to be *in the know,* so you won't make poor decisions based on wrong information. But how can you tell what the public mind, truth, and wisdom really are?

Wise teens will check out with trusted, informed

adults whatever they are hearing, seeing, or reading before assuming that's the way life really is nowadays. If and when you do so, be selective. Some peers and adults *go with the flow* when social trends first hit society, whether these trends are healthy or not. Many intelligent adults got into the pot and coke habit in the 1970s, and regretted it later.

If you want more than just your parents' opinions, ask other persons whom you respect—a favorite teacher, or a friend's parent.

Don't be afraid to ask; they will enjoy assisting you. Choose persons with good reputations who have built solid, happy lives for themselves. Grandparents and other older adults who have lived through a couple generations of social trends are particularly good choices. Time gives depth and strength to wisdom.

If you want to ask young adults, ask several whom you respect. There is greater wisdom in the judgment of many than in just one person's.

In-the-know Messages for Everyday Living

To build self-esteem, you need confidence about your personal appearance. It helps to know what society expects of you. You need to know how to take good care of yourself and how to be comfortable with your feelings. You need to feel capable of accomplishment and deserving of the respect of others.

You need to know how to get along well with people, and how to preserve your good feelings about yourself when you have conflicts with others. Your self-esteem grows as you build friendships and learn how to handle your adult sexuality. It helps your self-esteem to know how to handle the hard times of life gracefully.

The rest of the chapters of this book will put you *in the know* and will offer guidelines that have worked well for other teens to accomplish the above goals.

6.

I Want to Look Good

The famous singer and actress, Barbra Streisand, once wanted to have plastic surgery done on her hooked nose. However, the specialist she consulted told her that surgery might permanently change the distinctive sound quality of her vibrant soaring voice. Not wanting to risk an already successful musical career, Barbara did not have the surgery, but that decision did not hurt her professionally. She went on to play romantic leading roles with such prominent, handsome movie actors as Robert Redford.

* * *

You are or soon will be moving away from the security of your family to find a place of acceptance in the world. That's scary. Your parents *have* to accept you, because you were born into the family. The world is different. You have to make it on your own steam there. Since the first thing people notice about you is your body, you can't help but wonder, Do I look good enough?

As a teenager, you live in a changing body. That makes things even more difficult. Change, too, is frightening.

That change can come suddenly and unexpectedly. It's not unusual for a teen to shoot up six inches in less than a year. Adjusting to such rapid change can cause awkwardness. Many a teenager has tripped over furniture or run into a door. That adds another threat to self-esteem: embarrassment.

It's not surprising, then, that most teenagers are somewhat hung up about their bodies. But, as we saw with Barbra Streisand, even adults have problems with how they look. They are always dieting, changing their hair color, or wishing something about themselves were different. Part of the problem is that in today's world we are surrounded by unrealistic and impossible images.

Fighting Images

Society suggests that *beauty is everything,* especially for girls and women. At the same time, nobody can decide what *handsome* or *pretty* really is. Ask several people whom they think is the most beautiful female star on television. They'll give you several answers, probably no two alike. As Margaret Hungerford wisely said, "Beauty is in the eye of the beholder!"

Not only does our culture not agree on what beauty is; it also overrates its importance. You can't be fat. You can't be skinny. You have to look twenty years old whether you are thirteen or fifty, and your shape has to resemble that of Arnold Schwarzenegger or Christie Brinkley. And, heaven forbid, don't you *dare* have a blemish on your face!

Advertisements are everywhere—television, magazines, record covers, newspapers, billboards. One sees in them a standard that is not typical of human life. The tall, leggy female models have highly distinctive facial features. The men have muscular frames and a thick shock of hair. No one is bald, short, or potbellied.

In real life, people have frizzy hair, freckles, tubby trunks, beanpole legs, and knobby knees. One could say, Don't let the beauty craze affect you. But that is about as effective as having an ostrich protect itself by burying its head in the sand. We live in this world, and we have to deal with it.

How can you find self-esteem in a beauty-worshiping world? First, by giving yourself good messages about your body, whatever its shape and features. Second, by remembering that beauty depends just as much on what's within. Third, by knowing what is basic to a socially acceptable appearance. And fourth, by taking care of what God gave you to work with.

Accepting My Body

Believe it or not, it's not how you look but how you *feel* about how you look that makes or breaks your feeling good about yourself. Some of the best-loved movie and television stars (Michael J. Fox, Oprah Winfrey, Johnny Carson) have or have had less-than-perfect features or figures.

The secret is to accept your body. Are you shorter than normal? or taller? There's nothing wrong with that. When you think about it, most people are either one or the other. Very few people fall into the *average* category.

Julius Caesar was too short, and Abraham Lincoln too tall. Yet history found them admirable. Princess Diana towers over the average man. So does Brooke Shields. Dudley Moore is only five feet, two inches tall; yet he's popular with the most glamorous of tall women.

Fat or skinny bodies, plain or pretty faces, coarse or fine hair, curved or pointed noses, big or little ears – they're all normal. *Perfect* is not normal. All people get pimples once in a while, including your favorite movie or television star.

Are you proud of your body? You should be. Your body was given you by God as a framework. It is the foundation for what you are and what you will become. It is the physical structure on which your life hangs.

Any doctor will tell you that the human body is an enormously gifted object, deserving of the greatest respect. The capacity for seeing, hearing, smelling, tasting, and touching are all something to be thankful for. Those of us who have all of our senses in good working order are most blessed.

The detailed features that go with our bodies are ways of differentiating each of us from the other. We certainly don't all want to look alike! Those features that make us different from each other make us individuals.

If you are disabled, disfigured, or culturally different from the other people in your setting, you may have to try a little harder to give yourself good messages. You don't have the comfort of being one among many. There's no way you can blend in with the rest of the crowd.

Those who live with such circumstances and feel good about themselves say the best way to have poise is to be proud of what you are and have. Hold your head high. Accept as normal a certain amount of staring by others, realizing it is the starer's problem. Ignore or laugh about those occasional insensitive people who call attention to your differentness.

If you are so inclined, you can make life a bit easier for yourself and others by taking the initiative in introducing yourself. This helps them get over any initial hurdle and see the *you* below the surface a little faster.

The Truth About Beauty
True beauty comes more from what's inside than what's outside of us. Good feelings, positive attitudes, gestures of kindness, and concern for others make us beautiful people on the inside. They give us the serene and loving facial expressions and gestures that make us beautiful on the outside as well.

Everybody fell in love with physically ugly *E.T.* because he was such a lovable creature. The success of the television show, *Beauty and the Beast*, showed that many people could respond to the caring nature of the most inhuman-looking of creatures.

Neither perfect features nor perfect health are essential to a happy, satisfying life. In spite of blindness Stevie Wonder became one of America's most-loved singers. After teenager Joni Eareckson was left paralyzed from a diving accident, she learned how to paint pictures, became a best-selling author, and found love and marriage in spite of a permanent disability.

God, too, is more interested in the internal beauty. When he asked Samuel to anoint the young shepherd, David, to be Israel's king in place of the tall, handsome King Saul, he pointed out that men look at outward appearances, but the Lord looks at the hearts of people.

Looking Good Is Important When . . .

At the same time, we owe it to ourselves and others to care for what we have. Presenting our best self to others is important. It is courteous. Grooming and dressing well show respect for school, church, and other public groups. A good appearance will help you get the attention of that certain person in history class. Someday it will help you get that job you want. Here is what society requires for social acceptance:

- Bathe frequently—often enough to keep your body clean and smelling fresh. Especially cleanse the underarms, seat, and genital area. Shampoo your hair as soon as it gets greasy and keep it neatly brushed or combed. Use a deodorant daily or as often as is needed to avoid perspiration odor. (Perspiration and other body odors are not so much undesirable as they are overpowering for our modern society, where people are generally crowded into small rooms.)

- Launder your clothes, especially underwear and socks, whenever they are dirty or smelly. Keep your shoes relatively clean.

- To bring out the best in yourself, *dress in clothing that fits well and looks good* on your figure type. Try things on before you buy, to see how they look. The colors, designs, textures, lines, and shapes of clothes have different effects on different people. Vertical or horizontal stripes, large or small plaids, soft or stiff fabrics, and light or dark colors will give you different looks.

In color choices, watch for hair and skin color, especially of the face. Pale colors on fair-skinned persons can make them look ill. Redheads need to choose hues that blend with their strong natural coloring.

Avoid too much *busyness* in your dress. A bright plaid shirt worn with boldly printed shorts or pants can give a person a clownish look. And watch what colors you use together. Bright orange and raspberry red don't always look well together.

To Enhance My Appearance, What About . . . ?

- Acne? During adolescence, overworking skin glands prompt the appearance of blackheads and whiteheads, mostly on the face and back, for 80 percent of all teenagers. For some, acne becomes serious, lasting long after adolescence and causing major skin eruptions and scarring. The latter should be treated by a doctor, but for most teens acne is just a temporary aggravation. It can't be cured or prevented.

There are, however, several ways to reduce the symptoms of acne. Clean your skin with soap and water whenever it feels oily. Don't scrub it. Scrubbing irritates the skin and can make the acne worse. Avoid facial creams and tight-fitting clothes such as headbands and turtlenecks; they block the skin ducts. A little sunbathing and use of sunlamps may help clear up mild acne. So do certain nonprescription drugs, if you follow the instructions. If you need or want more help, doctors have several courses of treatment available.

- Suntanning? The sun-bronzed look is popular with many teenagers. However, too much exposure to the sun can not only make people sick, it can cause cancer and kill us.

Doctors recommend that, if you want or need to spend a lot of time in the sun, use a highly protective (high numbered) sunscreen lotion.

- Bodybuilding? Doctors say it is safe so long as you obtain supervision and/or follow the manufacturer's instructions for equipment usage. To avoid pulled muscles, work up gradually.

Steroid drugs, used in recent years to build up athletes for competition, are dangerous. They have several harmful side-effects. Doctors say, Don't use them—ever!

- Dieting is a common and potentially dangerous fad with many teenage girls. Many of the popular *trendy* diets are not good for health. Some are dangerous. Dieting can also get out of control. Thousands of young adults, including the rock musician Karen Carpenter, have died of anorexia, a dieting disorder that brings on starvation.

Doctors say teenagers rarely need to diet because their need for food energy is so high. Those teenagers who are truly obese and in need of food control should diet only under the care of a physician.

Self-esteem depends upon your feeling that you look good. But looking good also depends upon your feeling good, as we will see in the next chapter.

7.

I Need to Feel Good

Patty loved pretzels. One day she bought a whole pound to get her fill. She munched away like crazy until she was stuffed.

Half an hour later she didn't feel well. The pretzels did not come back up, but they didn't sit well on her stomach. She was uncomfortable for hours. She hated herself for pigging out. She also lost her taste for pretzels, permanently.

* * *

It's hard to feel good about yourself if you do yourself in, like my pretzel-eating friend did. Self-esteem requires that we take good care of our bodies. Since bodies are growing and changing fast during the teen years, giving them attention is especially important during this time.

Good health habits give people a sense of well-being, a zest for living, radiant smiles, peachy facial and skin tones, and piles of energy. Even persons with chronic health problems and disabilities reap many rewards from good care.

Poor health habits make us sluggish. Knowing that we have brought such yucky feelings upon ourselves depresses us. Poor habits also make us illness-prone. Do you remember how you felt the last time you had a cold? It was a far cry from the attitude that self-esteem brings: I am ready to take on the world.

When we don't feel well, we don't look good or act well either. Sick and health-careless people usually don't have the energy to stand erect, to groom themselves carefully, to think clearly, and to put in a good day's work with a smile.

What Makes for Good Health?

Teenagers need good eating, sleeping, and exercising habits.

Our bodies need a balanced diet of nutritious foods. The nutrients in foods enable us to grow strong and to repair and replace old and injured body tissue as well as ward off illness.

A good daily diet consists of three meals that contain something from each of the four basic food groups

- Breads, cereals, and other grains
- Fruits and vegetables
- Meat, fish, and poultry
- Milk or other dairy products

Add to this one extra serving each day from the grains, fruits or veggies, and milk groups.

It's not hard to get what you need, if you don't skip meals. Let's look at this typical menu:

- Breakfast: juice, cereal or toast, and milk
- Lunch: soup or fruit and a sandwich plus milk
- Supper: spaghetti with meat sauce, a roll, tossed salad, and milk

Supper contains two portions each of grains and vegetables. (The spaghetti and roll are both grains. The tomatoes in the spaghetti sauce and greens in the salad are veggies.) An extra glass of milk with any of the meals provides a fourth portion of dairy products.

You've already met the requirements, and you still have dessert and snacktime for some sweets, ice cream, pop, or whatever.

Nutritious food does not automatically make you healthy. You also need to maintain a desirable weight for your body frame. As we read in the last chapter, most teenagers don't need to diet. But those who are excessively overweight should diet as guided by a doctor. Obesity increases a person's chances of developing serious, permanent illness.

Since many factors go into weight control, and since anorexia (the starvation illness) is a real threat, your doctor is the best person to tell if you are too heavy. Your doctor can then put you on a safe diet.

Those persons who have other medical problems such as allergies or diabetes also need to follow their doctor's advice on the proper diet for their condition.

In-the-know Messages

- *Junk foods* such as candy and pop often get a bad rap. We call them *junk* because they have no value for our bodies. They usually do not hurt us. But they can become harmful if we consume them in such quantities that we do not eat enough of the healthful foods, or if they add too many calories or too much salt, sodium, fat, sugar, or chemical additives to our diet.

- *Fast foods* are okay, if you watch your food groups when you choose what you are eating. The calories tend to be high, but most teens can handle that unless they have an overweight problem. Watch out for too much fat or salt and not enough vegetables.
- Can't I just take *vitamins?* Some teens think that vitamin pills will take the place of healthful food. Not so. We need the solids and fibers in foods to move along smoothly the bodily processes of living, growing, moving about, and eliminating wastes.

Sleep, Blissful Sleep . . . What Is Enough?

All living things move in cycles of growing and resting—trees and other plants, animals, and people. During the rest times living things build energy that is needed for basic functioning. The need is sizable—80 percent of what is needed for active daytime living.

A national sleep research center found that all teens need at least nine hours of sleep a night. Some need more. Those who don't get it suffer bouts of drowsiness during the day. Sometimes teenagers watch television late into the night when they must be up for school the next day. Needless to say, they aren't going to function at their best. Fatigue depresses us.

Our bodies live by a certain rhythm. Air travelers to Europe and Asia know that because they experience jet lag. Staying up all night and then sleeping all the next day throws that rhythm out of balance for a time. A rare splurge will not harm a person seriously, but to feel well we need to respect that rhythm.

The Magic of Workouts

Our body's internal organs are working all the time. If they are to work efficiently, they need to be brought up to a good working speed regularly just like the engine of an automobile. What happens when the family car sits a long time or is used only for short bursts of city driving? Right! The motor gets clogged and needs a five- or ten-mile spin.

Aerobic exercises such as running, jogging, biking, and swimming give our heart and lungs a good workout. They race our body's internal engine, boosting the rate at which our foods turn into heat and energy (calories). Aerobic exercise helps us keep off excess weight by using calories at the same time it is decreasing our appetite.

The body's muscles need regular flexing so they aren't stretched or injured easily. Teens need thirty minutes of vigorous exercise daily. Gym classes usually provide this on the days students take gym, but that's not every day. Varsity sports make the grade for those students who participate. Some sports are not physically demanding, such as archery and bowling. Though they exercise a few muscles, they are not adequate for overall fitness.

One of the best ways to stay fit easily is to get into the habit of walking wherever and whenever you are able. Walk briskly. A slow saunter doesn't do much.

Exercise doesn't have to hurt, nor do you have to work hard at it. The best benefits come if you regularly work up to your physical limit for the recommended period of time. The amount of time depends upon the exercise. Putting in the time is more important than how you work at it.

Exercise gives us a natural high. The chemicals it releases in our body make us feel good afterward for several hours.

Sometimes teens get into sports so enthusiastically that they overdo. A nationally known physician says you know you are in too deep if you're having frequent sprains, muscle strains, or bone pain. Another way to tell is if you have no time for other pursuits, or if (for girls) menstruation is delayed.

Slouchy Sam, or Straight and Slim Steve?

It's normal during the years when your limbs are growing fast to feel awkward and ungainly. Rapid growth spurts don't give people time to adjust to the new proportions caused by their changing arm, leg, and body lengths.

Many teens respond to this change by slouching. If your body is hunched over, the internal organs cramp and cannot function as well as they should. A slouched, lumpy body doesn't look as good as a straight, upright one.

Standing straight and tall gives you a more graceful as well as confident appearance. Good posture will not stop or lessen tripping and other kinds of accidents that occur when rapid growth leaves you temporarily uncoordinated, but it won't make them worse. And it will make you feel better both physically and emotionally.

You can develop the good posture habit by visualizing yourself often as standing tall and sitting straight. Do so, even if you are a head above everyone else or feel like a dwarf in a room full of basketball stars. Persons with good posture look successful and confident. Then people don't notice size as much. They are too busy feeling good in turn.

Taking Care at Special Times

Feeling well also requires that you take care of yourself when illness strikes. A little extra rest when you are coming down with a cold can keep it from mushrooming into several days of misery. Similarly with other illnesses, the body will heal faster and the illness tend to be less severe if you rest more, exercise less, and eat nutritious foods as well as you are able during the illness.

Girls need to take good care of themselves during menstruation. Though this is a normal body process, it makes special demands on the body. The abdominal muscles cramp a bit because the uterus is contracting. Simple pain medicines usually take care of the discomfort. But it's also a good idea to avoid overexercising or getting chilled, as these can worsen the cramping.

Menstruating women who have severe pain, unexplainable mood swings, severe bloating, or other side effects should consult their doctor for a treatment program. Modern medicine has many ways to help them become comfortable, and comfort is important to one's sense of well-being.

Looking at Today's Teen Health

Teenagers in general in recent years have fallen into many poor health habits. They frequently skip meals, particularly breakfast (I got up too late!) and lunch (let's grab an ice-cream cone).

Some teenagers spend more time at the fast-food shop than at the family meal table. Others devour junk food and then find they are too full to eat regular meals. They often drink pop instead of milk at meals.

Milk is especially important in the teen diet, because its calcium aids strong bone growth. The adolescent years are important bone-building years. Some medical experts believe that the risk factors for bone and heart diseases start during the teen years. Unfortunately, almost half of today's teenage girls are consuming less than half the calcium they need. This could make them more prone to fractures or being a hunchback when they become older adults.

The physical fitness of today's teenagers is poor. A government survey in the mid-1980s found that most teenagers have a higher percentage of body fat than did the teens of earlier generations. They also performed more poorly on chin-ups, bent-knee sit-ups, and other tests measuring the body's overall fitness. Some of the biggest health-busters are too much television watching and riding rather than walking or biking to school.

The body you are building during your teenage years is the body that's with you for the rest of your life—possibly seventy years. Since you are the person who has to live with it, the best thing you can do is to develop a self-serving and God-pleasing attitude about your health. Make the decisions that are right for you.

This is not easy. We all like to follow the path of least resistance. It's simpler to follow the crowd than to do what is best. Nobody wants to stand out in the crowd, to be different. That doesn't feel good either.

There are times when you must break from the crowd. We'll talk about those times later, and about how to handle them. Occasionally breaking general health rules is not going to hurt you if you are basically healthy. But for maximum self-esteem you need to establish good, regular habits and stick with them.

Good Health Is Also . . .

For highest health and self-esteem, you need to take good care of your whole self. The apostle Paul wrote that your body is a temple of the Holy Spirit. He calls you to honor God with your body and your whole being (1 Corinthians 6:19-20). This involves not only your physical but also your mental, emotional, and spiritual health.

We take good care mentally when we exercise our minds and take an interest in the world around us. We take good care emotionally when we learn how to handle our feelings and develop positive attitudes. We take good care spiritually when we are true to our ideals and deal with our need for God.

In the next three chapters we will see how we can develop self-esteem in these other vital areas.

8.

I Want to Be Confident

In 1984 tall, smiling brown-haired Scott Schneider won a gold medal in the 100-meter dash, a silver in the 400-meter, and a bronze in the discus throw. In 1985, the lean, handsome young man won six gold medals, setting national records in five events and an international in the sixth. He was also on the championship soccer team. But it wasn't easy, because Scott falls down, on the average, twice a day every day of the year.

Scott won his medals from a wheelchair in the Olympic-style games for the disabled. Scott has muscular dystrophy. But he is determined to live a rich and full life in spite of it. "I think I'm very lucky having MD," he says. "It has caused me not to take things for granted, to live life to the fullest."

Grinning broadly, his warm brown eyes sparkling with excitement and genuine joy, Scott says he would prefer to be healthy if he had the choice, but he is enjoying the life he has. Scott is a graphic designer, artist, photographer, and public relations executive. He is also happily married and planning to raise a family.

* * *

Scott Schneider is confident. He found confidence by believing in himself in spite of his handicap, and by accepting the limitations of a physically restricted body. He found what he could do well and worked hard to build on those strengths. No small part of his success came from his positive mental attitudes.

You, too, can be confident by following the mental habits that Scott and other people with high self-esteem use—by working hard at realistic goals, by positive mental attitudes, by finding and developing your strengths, by giving yourself good messages when pressured by our competitive world, and by learning to deal with failure gracefully.

The Formula for Achievement

To reach any goal, one must be willing to work. Harvard University did a 40-year study of boys who grew up in poor and broken homes in inner-city Boston. Those who as youths had worked at home chores or in the community, regardless of their intelligence, income, race, or education, gained competence and came to feel like worthwhile members of society.

Try many things. Because you are entering or are in your early to midteens, lots of opportunities are open to you. Don't hesitate because you fear you might not do well. You will never know until you try. Fear can paralyze us, if we let it. Overcoming fear gives us self-confidence, even if we fail. And, it is just as important to find out what you *aren't* good at as what you are.

Be realistic in setting your goals. Scott wouldn't have made it to first base in the regular Olympics. The disabled athletes compete in four class ranges of games, based on degrees of difficulty with balance and musculature. Scott competed in the one for which he was qualified—the second strongest, Class Three.

You, too, need goals consistent with your abilities. We never achieve higher than our self-concept. So, set your goals high, but not out of sight.

Make yourself get going. The hardest part of doing anything is getting started.

Work hard, and be willing to overcome obstacles. Learning a new skill takes practice. Whether one's goal is acquiring piano dexterity or better tennis backhand shots, steady repetition improves performance.

The process may get tedious, but persisting pays off. Bart Starr, top quarterback of the Green Bay Packers during their golden years, became a star performer because of hours and hours of practice. He got tired and discouraged many times.

Use your failures as learning experiences. Thomas Edison tried 1,200 different materials for the filament of his incandescent light bulb before he found one that worked well.

Some self-criticism is healthy. Persons need to analyze what they could have done better in order to improve their skills. But don't overdo by hanging on to a loss, saying over and over, Oh, I should have done better! That's self-pity. Self-pity helps no one and drains away energy that could be put to good use elsewhere.

Mental Attitudes Make a Difference

Positive mental attitudes help greatly to determine whether we will reach our goals. "You have failed 1,200 times," an acquaintance once told Edison.

"I have not failed," he answered. "I have discovered 1,200 materials that won't work."

Winning requires believing in yourself. Former Miss Teenage America Becky Reid said that, when she started competing, "I was nervous, *not being my real self* ... and [for that reason] I couldn't succeed." When she changed her methods and did what she believed was right for *her*, she started to win.

Sometimes teenagers program themselves into poor self-esteem. They think or say, I'm dumb, or, That was stupid. They also program themselves to fail: I can't do it. I just know I can't. Programming yourself to fail is self-fulfilling. You will fail.

First Lady Eleanor Roosevelt once said, "No one can make you feel inferior without your consent." The opposite is also true. You can easily turn those kinds of messages around by replacing them with positive ones: I have ability in this, and I love doing it. I know I'll eventually be good at it.

Confidence also depends on you accepting your life situation as being okay, whether disabled like Scott, a member of a poor or divorced family, an only child, or whatever. There are benefits and drawbacks to all of life's circumstances. People rise above them. Some of the world's happiest music was composed in slavery by African American families celebrating something very precious that they owned—their love for God and each other.

Your circumstances are part of God's plan for your life. If they are good, you are lucky. If they happen to be difficult, sooner or later they will produce God's promised good. Marlo Thomas, movie and television star and daughter of the famous comedian Danny Thomas, said her father was on the road a lot. She used to think the telephone was part of his body and that theirs wasn't a *real* family. She found later that there are many kinds of families, and that the important thing is to love and share with each other—even by telephone, if necessary.

It's what you do with what God gave you that matters. A familiar saying goes, "Bloom where you are planted." The famous philosopher/columnist Sydney Harris once said, "Nobody has a right to take credit for what he or she was born with—only for what they have done with it."

Good mental attitudes call for us to recognize our talents and skills, but people with high self-esteem do not flaunt them. Everybody is turned off by braggarts. The idea is to be confident, not cocky. Confident people don't have to advertise their skills. They show.

Confident people do not deny their strengths, either. Sometimes to appear humble a winner will say, Aw, it was nothing. But accomplishment has value. People with high self-esteem don't want to deny themselves the value of what they do well. They say, Thank you, or, Yeah, I feel good about it. This was a hard one. Or something similar that is true and appropriate.

Finding and Developing My Strengths

You can tell early in grade school whether you are good at basic math and communication skills. As you get older, you need to focus on other and varied skill areas. Most school systems have testing programs in the upper grades to help you determine your specific areas of competence.

Generally speaking, your strengths relate closely to your interests. We soon lose interest in things we cannot do well. The guy who keeps missing pitched balls at the neighborhood park usually doesn't want to try out for the school baseball team. But if as a child he was always making up garage plays or singing in the shower, he might be great in the school play or choir.

If school work comes hard to you, choose subjects that match your natural abilities. One high schooler with poor English but strong mechanical skills took a mechanics class in school and, as part of a cooperative business program, worked afternoons in a service garage. Another took a lot of music classes, eventually becoming a band teacher.

Don't hesitate to change your sights, if you find a promising new interest. That mechanics student took chemistry his last year of high school and loved it. In spite of the limited language skills that dogged him all through graduate school, he went on to obtain a doctorate in organic chemistry.

The noted psychologist, James Dobson, suggests that, to firm up confidence in yourself, learn to do one thing well. He chose tennis. Somebody else might choose needlecraft. One young person I know (not an *A*-student) is a speed reader. She draws fifteen books out of the public library every week and reads them all.

Are Good Grades Necessary?

Some teenagers with limited scholastic ability call themselves dumb. Philosopher Sydney Harris said, "Everybody is dumb about different things in different ways."

Some abilities can't be tested on a piece of paper or with equipment. Some students are bright, but don't handle tests very well. And, as the mentally handicapped Bennie on the television show *L. A. Law* shows, even persons with limited intellectual ability have much to offer society.

If your strengths are not in school subjects, can you just let school work go, chalking it off as "my weakness"?

Yes, and no.

Yes, grades are important. You can't feel good about yourself if you goof off. Some people have to work harder in school than others to get acceptable marks, but that doesn't mean that a person shouldn't try.

Second, learning is never lost. It's a precious asset that is with you for life. The more a person learns, the more interesting life becomes. Applying that learning makes us wiser, and thus able to build better lives.

Third, the working world looks at education as a measure of a person's capabilities. It's hard to get a job without a high school diploma. In modern society, technical school or college training is almost a necessity to get the better jobs.

Yet, grades aren't everything, though they are important. Top grades aren't essential for many trades such as mechanics, plumbing, typing, or waitress work. Nor are all *A*-grades a *must* for college, though good grades are.

Some teenagers are under heavy pressure to get top grades. They drive themselves. Or their parents, wanting the best for them, apply pressure. Some prestigious colleges require top grades. But our lives need a balance of work and play, pressure and relaxation. The cost has to be weighed.

Confidence and self-esteem do not come from excessively hard work and pressure. They come from honestly doing one's best and being satisfied with the results, while at the same time living a balanced life.

Good Messages for a Competitive World

We live in a world flooded with competition. Businesses compete. Television networks compete. Professional sports teams compete. Politicians running for office compete.

High school sports teams compete. Team members compete for starting positions. Band players compete for performance awards and for the first chair in their sections. Debate teams compete.

We can't even get away from competition in social events. Halloween parties have contests for the best witch and ghost costumes. Monopoly and video game players compete.

Sometimes there are several notches in the competition. Only one can win. That means a lot of people are going to be losers. Losing doesn't feel good. Coming in last feels awful. But somebody has to be last.

How can a person be confident in such a world?

Because we never perform at a level higher than our self-concept, it's important to keep a positive image of ourselves high in our minds at all times: I have God-given talents. I will do what God wants me to with them—no more, and no less. They will have value, because God doesn't waste things.

If losing bothers you a lot, don't set yourself up to lose. Don't go out for the baseball team if you know you are not well-coordinated. Don't try out for choir if you are tone deaf. You can always fulfill any love you have for baseball or singing by indulging your passion with your family and friends.

When you are in a losing situation, give yourself positive messages. Think to yourself, I know I have ability in this area. I've done well before. This is just an off day. If losing in a field in which you are not strong, tell yourself, I didn't expect to win. I only played to have fun. Or, I only took part because I had to. Or, whatever the truth is.

When Others Taunt

Plump Denise bent over in school to pick up a book that had fallen. Some boys behind her, eying her buttocks, said, "Wow! What hams!" Denise's face turned bright red and she ran out of the room in tears.

Jim was practicing basketball with a couple of buddies in gym during a free period. One of them tripped him on purpose and jeered at him, right in front of girls practicing at an adjacent backboard.

Confidence derails fast when one runs into this kind of thoughtlessness, meanness, or cruelty from peers. There are three major ways of handling these kinds of situations:

- Pulling yourself together and then *walking away quietly* is the easiest way. It's also graceful. It maintains your dignity. And it immediately stops the crass behavior.
- Some people might want to *confront the*

teasers: "How would you feel if it were you?" The problem with this option is that it might spur the teaser to keep going: "Wouldn't bother me a bit!" The best answer to that is, "It bothered me."

If you are going to confront, avoid carrying things too far. The teasing could go on and on: "Aw, now she's getting touchy." Or, "Jimmy can't take a little kidding!" The taunting game won't stop until someone gets tired of it or until the victim, refusing to be humiliated further, stops it by walking away.

The Values of Humor

• A third way of handling the situation would be to *make light of it*. Denise could have said, "Yeah, guess I gotta get me on a diet." Or, "Thanks for noticing." Jim could have said, "That's some way to get a guy to fall for a girl."

A sense of humor helps in many of life's difficult situations. People generally respond better to joking than to tears.

But that's not the greatest value of laughter. A sense of humor puts things in perspective. Denise felt terribly humiliated. But the only damage done was that she was temporarily the brunt of a little cruel but minor teasing. For Jim the incident, though unkind, only resulted in a little embarrassment.

Humor also heals. People get over hurt feelings fast when they can laugh and make light of the situation.

A sudden, unexpected emotional outburst from yourself can undermine your confidence. So does having to look in the mirror the next morning, after you have sneaked a beer at a friend's house.

The next two chapters deal with our emotional and spiritual selves and needs.

9.

I Want to Be Comfortable with My Feelings

Sarah promised her mother she would clean her room on Saturday. On Thursday her friend Michelle invited her to go shopping Saturday. Sarah thought about doing the cleaning on Thursday night, but Thursday was a good television night. She thought about doing it on Friday night, but she came home tired. Everybody needs to relax after a long week, she told herself.

Saturday dawned, and Sarah's work was not done. "You can't go shopping," her mother said.

Sarah exploded. "*Why not?* I can do it later. It's *my* room anyway! Why should *you* care what it looks like?"

"You made a promise, Sarah."

Sarah moped around all day, dejected.

* * *

Have you ever felt like Sarah? If so, you are not unusual. All people disappoint themselves at times.

It takes more than belief in our abilities to give us confidence and self-esteem. Part of our makeup consists of our emotions, or feelings. They impact heavily on our health and mental state. Doctors believe that at least half of their patients' illnesses are caused by emotional or stress-related problems.

People with high self-esteem know that feelings are important. They respect their body's reactions and the need to deal with strong pleasant and unpleasant feelings. Since maximum good feelings come from good emotional health habits, they also know and try to follow those.

About Feelings

Feelings are energy responses that well from deep within us. They come from the heart. They are traffic signs, asking for matching actions. A positive feeling like elation makes one want to jump up into the air: Oh, wow, did I ever do good on that test today! A negative feeling like grief might cause tears and depression: Grandma died today. Angry feelings sometimes lead to fights.

Negative feelings, the ones that make us uncomfortable, are not necessarily bad. God got angry, and so did Jesus. Feelings are not right or wrong in themselves. They do not cause us trouble, but the actions that follow them can.

Some people think they cannot keep from acting out their feelings. Wrong. Feelings are not actions. They are the emotions that sometimes lead to actions. But we can stop before we act. Managing the expression of one's feelings is important. More than one player and even coaches have ruined careers in football because they couldn't hold their tempers and got into brawls.

Our thoughts determine our feelings. There is a wide gulf between thinking and acting upon those feelings. Have you ever thought, I'd like to knock so-and-so's block off! Thinking about it didn't make it happen or bring it anywhere close to happening. (But mulling over that thought could build up more inner steam. We might find it harder to resist the temptation.)

We can react to feelings in satisfying ways. Instead of knocking that person's block off, you might decide to talk to that person about the incident that made you so mad. Or, if it was just an accident that caused momentary pain, you might decide to let it go and forget about it.

Some people show their feelings openly. It isn't hard for others to see how they feel. They laugh, cry, and blow their tops easily. Others hold their emotions inside. One can only tell how they feel by asking them questions. These are different ways of responding to feelings. Neither way is right or wrong in itself, but we do need to consider the effect on ourselves and others. What tears down? What is helpful and useful?

Feelings are important. Those arising from love are probably the greatest feelings in the world. Where would we be without them? Sensing rejection—not being wanted or accepted by others—is probably the worst. Is anything in life harder to swallow?

Many experts say that the most important decisions in life (shall I marry this person? should I move to a new community?) are best based on our deepest feelings. The answers have to meet the needs of the heart as well as mind.

Characteristics of Feelings

Feelings are fleeting. They don't last long. You may be down in the dumps after an argument with a parent one minute, and a few moments later be ecstatic after a phone call from *that special person.* Dramatic ups and downs are common with teenagers.

Feelings alone can do us in if we let them run our lives. They need to be filtered through the thinking process to do the best job for us. Everybody has purchased a piece of clothing impulsively at one time or another, and then regretted it later. It didn't fit. Or that person had nothing to wear it with.

The emotions of a group of people, unsifted by thought, can be treacherous. Lynch mobs, carried away by their feelings, execute people without fair trials.

Feelings come in all kinds of disguises. You may not immediately recognize twisted reactions to feelings. You might yell at your sister when you are really mad at the teacher who assigned too much homework that night.

Feelings aren't always reliable. When Brian got mad at his best friend, Tom, he ran to his room and wouldn't come out. He let his dad enter his room an hour later, but turned his back. Finally he blurted out, "I feel so lonely."

The feeling of loneliness was real. Brian felt isolated from others. But the feeling was not reliable. His father was there, caring, ready to enter Brian's world when Brian was ready. Behind the feeling, Brian was telling himself something that did not fully square with reality.

Feelings are real. Sometimes people deny them, saying, I'm not angry! . . . That gossip didn't hurt me. . . . I'm not jealous. . . .

If the feelings are real but denied, they will emerge in other ways. Persons truly angry will raise their tone of voice and, if the anger is great, may pound a table, wall, or another person with their fists. People who are hurt speak with sad resignation and slump in their chairs. The jealous get indignant in denying the truth.

Denying feelings does not control them, since they come out anyway sooner or later in body language or in acts of built-up frustration, as shown above. Recognizing them and directing their expression is more satisfying.

Feelings Common to Teens

It's normal for teens to have inconsistent desires for freedom. One day you like being dependent on your parents. The next day you want to make your own decisions.

The changes going on in your life bring with them loneliness and fear, caused by insecurity. You don't know exactly what to expect, or when. One acquaintance of mine began to develop breasts at the age of eight. A woman friend did not grow hers until her mid-twenties, after she became pregnant. Others don't always understand how it feels to be an early bird or a late bloomer. Late bloomers fear they will never be *normal.*

Your need to begin to take independent action can bring on loneliness and fear. Because the road you are traveling is a solitary one, it is lonely. Because your route has been untraveled by you or anyone else, it can be a bit frightening.

As you break away from your family, misunderstandings often occur. They isolate you from those who most want to love and support you. You think, Can't they see how I feel? Isolation, too, is fearful.

Ways of Coping

It helps to note that almost all teens experience these feelings, to a lesser or greater extent. The process is universal, even though your specific journey is not. In 1985 a teenager wrote Ann Landers, "I appear confident and capable of handling anything, [but] actually I have many fears." She enclosed a survey showing how 465 teenagers shared 18 different fears in varying degrees.

Straight thinking helps to put feelings into perspective. You may think you're the only teen ever to have been embarrassed because your brassiere strap broke in school. Is it true? Logic says it must have happened to many other girls. How important is it? Chances are, no one else in school noticed except the best friend you told and the gym teacher who gave you a safety pin.

It helps to remember that unpleasant feelings are temporary. Nothing remains the same for long. Whether you are disappointed, embarrassed, or humiliated, time removes the pain. An added bonus: bystanders forget about our bad moments much faster than we do.

Dealing with Feelings

Identifying your feelings will help you deal with them. It tells you what's really bothering you.

Where your feelings are strongest, that's where the most energy or serious problem lies.

Joe came home from school in a sour mood, complaining about homework. But when his father got home and asked him about football practice, he blew up. He pounded on the countertop and ranted and raved for several minutes about how bad the team was.

Then the truth came out. Joe had missed several tackles at football practice and had been knocked off the starting team for Saturday's game. The homework was a concern, but Joe's greatest distress was about not doing well at football practice.

Most people find it helpful to give the feeling a name and note how strong it is. Joe was *disappointed* about something he valued. He had *failed* to make the starting team. His extreme disappointment was justifiable. Naming the feeling and owning it is usually freeing and makes for less trouble.

As we said earlier, we can control how we act on our feelings. We handle emotional moments by giving ourselves a little time and space. Some people want a few minutes alone in their room, others a walk that burns off intense feelings, and others escape into a novel, movie, or television show.

Time and distance help us get a grip on ourselves. They also allow us to see the problem more clearly. Sometimes that alone satisfies our needs. Other times we have to plan changes in our habits or relationships. Or we may need to use up energy from the feeling in some constructive manner.

There are several ways to disperse intense feelings. Vigorous physical activity such as roller-skating, punching a pillow, or scrubbing floors is especially helpful. Some people write letters or essays until the feelings come out. Others write poetry.

It honors God and is important to our self-esteem to direct our strong feelings in harmless ways. Joe was mad that he missed those tackles—so mad that he wanted to punch in his locker door. But that could have injured his hand. Instead, he slapped away at the shower wall with his towel for several minutes and then ran all the way home.

Fear, Anger, Guilt, and Loneliness

The four uncomfortable feelings that cause people the most trouble are fear, anger, loneliness, and guilt.

The best way to work through fear is to learn all you can about the thing you are afraid of. Step out with courage and take the risks required to conquer it. If the fear is so intense that it prevents you from leading a normal life, get professional help. You can learn to get on top of it.

We work through anger by confronting it. Earlier we learned some ways to vent our feelings when we are angry with ourselves. If we have angry feelings toward others too strong to overlook, we need to talk to them. Chapter 12 will show you how to resolve conflicts with others.

We work through guilt by accepting God's forgiveness, forgiving ourselves, and making amends. We will discuss this in the next chapter.

Loneliness is with us off and on throughout life. We conquer it by finding listeners. Sharing your feelings with a trusted relative or friend is an excellent way to dissipate them. As you talk through frustrations, anger, joys, and disappointments, their intensity lessens, making them easier to handle. Putting things into words also helps you to see what's wrong and explore different ways of handling it.

Write down on the *My Listeners* page at the back of this book the names of all the people who care about you—friends, parents, sisters and brothers, pastor, church school teachers, public school teachers, grandparents, aunts and uncles and their families, neighbors, and other acquaintances.

This is your support group. Any of these people could be of help to you under certain circumstances. Look at your list during those times when you need to share. Add to it the names of any new caring acquaintances and friends you make.

Sometimes other people's needs collide with ours. They don't have time for us when we need it. Someone on that list wants to share with you. Keep trying until you find a listener with open time. If your need is urgent, say so. Most friends will take the time, if they know that.

To Create Better Feelings

We can program ourselves toward having better feelings in troublesome situations. We do this by changing the way we think about them. Joe knew the competition for the first-string tackle positions would be tough. He also knew there were a lot of good players, and that he sometimes missed hits.

He would not have been as disappointed had he told himself, I would like to play a lot, but I am not that good and I probably won't. I will be happy just to sit on the team. Or he could have said to himself, My goal is only to take in the practice and work together as a team. That's a good goal.

Programming has to be truthful. It wouldn't work for Joe to program himself to be satisfied with second string if he doesn't believe it's okay to be there. The idea is to image oneself as happily doing that job. And one has to persist at this kind of emotional programming, if it is to succeed. Joe needs to imagine himself several times a day as sitting on the bench, happy to be there.

For maximum self-esteem, programming also has to be positive. He may convince himself, I'll be a second-string tackle and be happy with that. But if that is just because he is too lazy to practice hard, he is not living up to his best capabilities. Less than one's best never satisfies.

Good Emotional Health Habits

For good emotional health, people with high self-esteem try to follow these guidelines:

- Enjoy today. You'll never have another chance at it. Do not let yesterday's anger or tomorrow's fear keep you from doing your best with the present moment and day.

- Enjoy the simple things around you. Flowers. Rocks. Birds. Mosses. Stones. People who use all their senses—seeing, hearing, smelling, tasting, and feeling—to enjoy whatever is around them, see every day of life as a fascinating adventure.

- Enjoy people. Hibernating in your own nest does not bring happiness for long. Look outside yourself. Support others. Seek them out when you need a friend.

- Keep yourself busy with physical and creative activity. Whether schoolwork, chores, sports, or a hobby—productive activity affords us the joy of doing something of value.

- Don't look for a knock in your motor. Some people are forever miserable, always looking to see if they hurt somewhere. Take care of any concerns you have about your health promptly, but don't go looking for them.
- Be decisive. Decide what you are going to try, do it, review it, and then quit thinking about it. Take a chance, even if you are wrong. Indecision, like self-pity, drains emotional energy without accomplishing anything.
- Be cheerful. You can be grumpy, or accepting of whatever life throws your way. Your disposition is something you decide.

10.

I Want to Be a Good and Honorable Person

Tim and Bob were good friends. Both played on the school's basketball team. They also groaned together over Shakespeare and Chaucer in the same English class.

The school had an *honor code,* meaning that all students were required to hold each other accountable for honesty in the classroom. During a particularly hard test, Tim noticed that Bob was peeking at notes stuffed up his sleeve.

Under the honor code, it was his duty to report Bob to the teacher. But he also knew that Bob needed a good grade to stay on the team. The team needed him to win. What should he do? Which was more important, his obedience to the school code or his loyalty to Bob and the team?

* * *

Goodness comes from making healthy moral choices about what is right or wrong—ones that are good for you and society. Honor comes by living up to those choices. But sometimes that is very hard to do. Should you turn in a cheating friend? Which is more important, obedience or loyalty?

Finding Standards to Live By

All around us in the world today we see signs of ethically questionable behavior. People walk over other people, sometimes without even realizing it. People grab what they want, pushing others aside. Bosses hire their cronies and fire others, callously disregarding the rights of their employees.

Workers steal company money and time by filching supplies and calling in sick when they are not ill. Craftsmen and construction workers do substandard work to pad profits, and people are cheated or killed. Politicians run into charges of improper actions. Professional criminals rake in millions through drug dealing, prostitution, gambling, and pornography—ventures that savagely mutilate the lives of people.

And society in general has taken on an *anything-goes* moral climate.

Most of your input about moral values comes from your mom and dad, who got most of theirs from their moms and dads. If your parents have lived a good life, most of their ideas will work well for you. But the role of your parents is limited. Parents aren't perfect. They make mistakes. They argue. Some get divorced. Besides, you are living in a different time from them. The temptations are not the same.

The world we live in today doesn't always have good models. Sometimes people look like faithful servants. They worship God and help each other in times of distress (depression, earthquakes, accidents). Then later they forget God and cheat each other when there is material prosperity.

Your self-esteem is only as high as your standards are reliable. Not only must standards give people a good life, they must also be firm and well-grounded. Where can you find standards like that? Where does your conscience fit in? How do you handle the problems when you choose wrong? And where can you find the strength to live by your principles in a morally loose world?

How to Live Right

God gave us the best standard there is in the Ten Commandments (Exodus 20). They describe our healthy response to God's help, and they really work. They've been around for almost 3,300 years, and no other religion has come up with a better, more workable set of rules to live by.

The Commandments show people how to keep their priorities straight and how to get along with each other. First of all, recognize and honor your Creator as the guiding light in your life. Who better than the Creator of life knows how best to live that life?

Second, and just as important, behave toward others with love, kindness, fairness, equality, and respect. That's the best way to get along. An easy way to remember this is with the golden rule: Treat others as you would have them treat you (Matthew 7:12).

All of Scripture is useful in guiding us in living

rightly. And God's Spirit speaks through his people to help us understand the Bible..

God also reaches us through our consciences. We are accountable for our actions—all of them. If you want to do what is right and what God wants for you, decisions for things not God-pleasing will leave you uneasy. If you go ahead anyhow and act on those decisions, you will feel miserable about what you have said or done.

I'm Not So Bad, Am I?

Some people think that, if they aren't in trouble with the law, they are living a pretty good life. God expects more from us than that. He wants us to obey all of the Commandments, all of the time. They were written for our good. If we don't follow them consistently we are not living up to the best in us.

Most of us want to live a good life. But wanting is one thing, doing is another. It's not easy to control your sexuality in a world where temptation is thrown at you, everywhere you go. It's not easy to be content with little in a world where wearing the latest styles and owning the state of the art in electronic equipment is the *in* thing with teens.

Mouthing off at parents or a teacher, gossiping, envy, jealousy, and thinking themselves better than others—these are some of the other sins even obedient God-fearing teenagers sometimes get caught up in. At the root of most of them is a lack of self-esteem.

Messages that remind you that you are a unique person created by God with gifts to be used for his special purposes—these help you rise above temptation by making it unnecessary for you to gain the attention or envy of others. The more you keep giving yourself this good news, the more quickly you yourself will come to believe it and the easier it will be to live by it.

Wanting control, or wanting one's own way, is another big problem—with everybody. The lovebooks author, Leo Buscaglia, says it is the main cause of trouble between people. Psychologist James Dobson agrees. Who of us doesn't prefer his or her own ideas and interests over someone else's? Sometimes we even take advantage of others, to get our way.

Hard Decisions

To hold to good moral standards, teens may have to make hard decisions. Turning in a cheating friend is a hard decision because it calls for *tough love*.

In the story at the beginning of this chapter, the greatest kindness Tim could do for Bob would be to ask him to turn himself in. This way Bob, who is causing the problem, has to take responsibility for it. It would also eventually help Bob's self-esteem, as self-esteem does not come from never making mistakes. Instead, it arises from taking full responsibility for one's actions, whatever that might cost us.

Sometimes hard moral decisions call for us to stand alone. Moments such as when a friend wants us to get into drugs or shoplifting are difficult, but not impossible. One can give the friend an answer that won't offend, and then walk away: Sorry, Jim, this isn't for me. Or just leave without saying anything.

It's better and easier to make those decisions

well in advance. You do that by choosing your friends carefully and by avoiding questionable situations, if and when someone in your group suggests them.

I Am One of the Chosen

The highest possible self-esteem comes from knowing that, even though we are and will continue to be imperfect, we who are God's followers have been found acceptable and are wanted by our loving Lord. In one of Jesus' parables, the Good Shepherd left his flock of 99 to search for one sheep who was lost. That's how precious each of us is to him. That one sheep could be you, or me.

How do you know if you are one of the chosen? Do you want to be? Then you can. His door is open to all who want to come in.

Because we are accepted by Jesus, we can forgive ourselves when we do wrong. Jesus long ago paid for our shortcomings. All he wants from us is to feel sincere regret, ask his forgiveness, and accept the fact that he has already forgiven us. If we have caused a problem for someone else, we must also do what we can to make things right for that person.

Feeling sorry about what happened is not hard. Remorse comes easily. But many people have a great deal of trouble accepting the fact that they did wrong. They can't accept their guilt and Jesus' forgiveness because they can't see themselves as faulty human beings.

People with high self-esteem admit their guilt. They realize that a perfect God is willing to accept them as they are, complete with mistakes. God knows they are going to have slipups even while heading in the right direction. Thus we too ought to accept ourselves just as we are.

Jesus came to earth and endured the cross so that we could be forgiven and put our mistakes behind us. To do this, we need to forget about the offense. We aren't looking ahead if we keep saying for days, "Oh, if only I hadn't. . . !"

In addition to trusting God's forgiveness, it is often freeing for us to confess our sins to other trusted believers. Then we can pray for each other and assure each other of God's forgiveness (James 5:16).

Letting go of the guilt frees us to become more effective for God in the world. Guilt, like indecision and self-pity, consumes a lot of energy that doesn't do anyone any good. Spending that energy elsewhere, such as on the urgent needs of other people, makes us much happier and better persons than carrying guilt around.

Other people will like you better, too, if you admit you are human and make mistakes. They are more comfortable with you. Think about two or three people whom you like very much. Isn't this true with them?

Improving My Bad Habits

Owning up to our shortcomings and working on them helps our self-esteem. Does that surprise you? It's true. Admitting we are human, faulty creatures takes the pressure off us to be perfect. Then we are mentally able to move ahead and make improvements in ourselves. It feels good to see that happening.

It's hard for us to recognize our bad habits because we don't like to look at them. To spot yours, take a mental note of what you say or do that regularly annoys people.

Quiz yourself on these common shortcomings: Am I always finding fault with others? Do I habitually talk about people behind their backs? Do I plot to get back at them after they hurt me? Do I keep hanging on to my anger and throw verbal darts at people instead of forgiving?

Also note the things you do that bother *you*, causing you to feel bad about yourself. Possible examples: procrastination, laziness, carelessness, and jealousy.

To get rid of these habits, pray for God's help and work on them. Pray as if everything depended on God, and work as if everything depended on you. In time you'll find that, with God's help, people are able to rise above many common failings.

Forgiving Others

Other people, especially those we live with, have habits that irritate us. Occasionally an acquaintance or even a friend is nasty. All of us human beings are hard to live with fifteen percent of the time, and impossible about five percent. With some people, the figures are much higher.

People who get along well tolerate the difficult fifteen percent and confront the offender about the impossible five percent. You'll learn how to do that in chapter 12.

To feel good about ourselves, we need to forgive others when they hurt us. We need to see them as *okay* people, too, in spite of their mistakes. God does not want us to judge them. In his eyes, no one person is better than another. We all have our five percents.

Experts have found that you have to forgive yourself before you can forgive others. Maybe that's why people have so much trouble with it. Jesus said, "Forgive others, even as I have forgiven *you.*" There lies the secret. If we can accept *Jesus'* forgiveness for *us,* we can forgive others.

Is Faith Important?

God's forgiveness does not reach everybody. Does that shock you? It's true. It is offered to everybody. But it isn't ours until we ask for it. We don't really feel good about ourselves until we have it. That takes faith.

Many teens question their faith in God. This is normal. It is also healthy. Without mentally testing the faith of your parents and the other spiritual leaders of your childhood, you can not have a faith of your own.

People can live without faith. They can also handle trouble, to a point, without faith. But people can not begin to fully appreciate God's creation, or his forgiveness, or the greatness of his love until they have made their peace with God.

People, even some of God's people, tend to rely on themselves when all is going well. We wait for his guidance until we need him. Thus we miss out on some of his greatest blessings.

The peace of God can bring a bedrock of inner joy, no matter what problem life brings, what evil is going on around us. And lasting self-esteem comes with knowing I have been found worthy by the only Being to whom I truly owe something, the one who owns me because he created me.

We need the strength that comes from God. Sometimes we are weak. Especially today, with moral decay around us, God can provide unlimited resources to help us deal with the hard decisions we may have to face and difficult actions we may have to take in life.

Can you, a just-emerging adult, have a real, vital, meaningful faith? Jesus told his followers that the best kind of faith is like the faith of a child. How do you get it? Jesus said that all we have to do is accept him and his love and seek his will for our lives.

Just like our bodies, our souls need to be fed so we can know and follow that will. God teaches us his will through the Bible. He guides us as we pray to him. The church is God's arm, working in the world to feed our faith and help us grow by offering worship, fellowship with his people, and communion.

The Joy of Doing for Others

Jesus summarized the Ten Commandments by saying, "Love the Lord your God with all your heart, your soul, your mind, your strength," and, "Love your neighbor as yourself" (Mark 12:30-31). We cannot ever fully repay God's love for us directly. But Jesus said we can return it in part by sharing ourselves and the resources he gives us with those in need around us—the poor, the hurting, the sick, and the lonely. Faith in action helps us be a part of the goodness that gives light and hope to our sometimes dark, cruel world.

Some teenagers ask, Will my small efforts to help others matter? When Samantha Smith, the young Maine schoolgirl, wrote a letter to Soviet leader Yuri Andropov, she bridged a cold war between two giants and fueled the movement for peace.

Over the centuries, thousands of Christians in quieter ways have been God's instruments to improve society with hospitals, schools for the deaf, and homes for the poor and mentally ill. Every time you visit patients in a nursing home or donate to a food pantry, you are sharing God's goodness with the world.

11.

Getting Along with People

Betty got mad when Mary didn't meet her downtown at 3:00 p.m., as planned. When Mary arrived around 4:00 p.m., Betty turned a cold shoulder and walked off. The next day Betty found out that Mary thought they had agreed to meet at four.

When Bob was roughhousing with Dick in the gym, Dick knocked him against the concrete gym wall. "Ya jerk!" Bob yelled, holding up a scraped elbow. After school, he tripped Dick as he was coming out the door.

Denise wanted a new sweater. Her mom said no. So when her mom was out, she cozied up to her dad and asked him. She knew her dad couldn't say no to her. When Denise's mother returned home, the mother was furious.

* * *

Good relationships with other people are our greatest source of joy, happiness, and comfort in living. Bad ones cause our greatest distress. Thus our self-esteem depends heavily upon our getting along well with others. You can't feel good about yourself when you've had a misunderstanding with a friend or a fight with Mom or Dad.

Why I Need Others

It's good to bounce our thoughts and ideas off other people. It can be very revealing to look beyond our own limits and see what others see. Mary asked Linda if she liked her new sweater and skirt. Linda thought it would look better if Mary wore a printed scarf with it—one that would blend the colors. Mary was delighted with the results.

We need company to share fun and for comfort. When you get good news, what is the first thing you want to do? When you read a really good book, how do you feel if nobody wants to hear you tell about it?

If someone in your class at school snubs you, would you rather go off by yourself and sulk, or find a sympathetic ear somewhere? Which way lifts you the most when you are in a funky mood? People also help to meet our needs. That's what support groups are all about. You are lonely, so you ask a friend to come over and visit.

Why Don't We Get Along?

As you know well by now, people have different ways of looking at things and doing things. No one person's way is the right answer for everybody. My best friend likes to "go with the flow." I like to think things through before acting on them. Neither of us is wrong. There is value in both ways.

People also may have tunnel vision. They can't see the other person's way, only their own.

Everybody wants his or her own way. Since that won't work, everybody wants his interests put first. The courts are full of neighbors fighting over line fences. Most of life's conflicts—parent-teen, friend-friend, union-management, or spouse-spouse—are simply power struggles. The one wins who shouts the loudest, makes the most ruckus, or holds out the longest.

The best way to get along with others is to follow the golden rule. Treat others as you would have them treat you. Put yourself in the other person's shoes and ask, How would *I* feel about this? If Betty had asked Mary why she was late, she would soon have found they had simply had a misunderstanding about the time. Had the tables been turned, she would have wanted Mary to trust her.

It is also important to be reasonable in your expectations of others. Nobody's perfect. If Bob had thought through the incident with Dick, he would have realized it was an accident.

We get along better if we open ourselves to the ideas of others. Dan was making a pizza. His mom suggested he make it with a thick crust. Dan didn't listen. He wanted a crisper, flat edge. While the pizza was baking, the sauce bubbled over onto the oven floor. Mom was mad because there was a smelly mess in the oven. Dan was mad because he had to clean it up.

Good Manners

Good manners oil the machinery of human relationships, preventing or minimizing conflicts. They also build good feelings between people.

Gulping down your food too fast, belching, and wiping your nose on your shirt sleeve turn people off, including your peers. So do wearing dirty clothes and appearing straggly bearded or unshaven, especially with dark hair. Playing your boom box too loud in public places annoys others. Cursing is a breach of courtesy as well as an offense to God; it grates on the ears of God's followers.

Many teens use these behaviors to gain attention. They get attention, but not the right kind. Courtesy shows respect, thoughtfulness, and consideration for others. We use silverware so that we don't gross out people by messing our clothes, hands, or the floor. Introducing strangers avoids awkwardness for them. *Please* gives the other person the right to say no and *thank you* tells people we appreciate the fact that they have put themselves out for us.

Asking before you take a second serving of pie assures there will be enough for all those who want more. Giving elderly or handicapped persons room to get by you on the sidewalk saves them from possible accidents and injury.

Some guys fend off good manners as *sissified*. They aren't. Manners take time and energy. Those who don't bother to learn and use them are telling other people they are not worth their time or caring.

Do you use good manners? If you aren't sure, ask your parents and/or a close friend.

Healthy Interaction

To get along well, we need to interact with each other in healthy ways. When Denise cozied up to her dad, she was manipulating him. She wasn't proud of herself. Her mom was mad. And her dad was disgusted, too, when he realized what had happened.

It works better to be straightforward. Denise's mother might have reconsidered if Denise had told her *why* she wanted the sweater and her mom had realized how badly Denise wanted it. As it was, Denise never did like that sweater.

It's important to know when *not* to speak. If you are afraid of offending people by your remarks, don't make them. Do you really *have* to tell Krista that her blouse doesn't look good on her? If she wants to know, she'll ask. Before you speak, think about what you want to say before you say it. Go off by yourself for a few minutes, if you need to. Time taken before speaking often saves trouble and misunderstanding.

When people pressure you, ask for time. Don't commit yourself before you are ready to make a statement or decision:

"How about it, Bill? Will you be equipment manager for the track team? I have to know today."

"I'm interested, but I need time to think about that."

If someone asks you a question and you don't know the answer, say so. You say you don't want to appear dumb? You aren't. Just honest. Your self-esteem does not depend on your having to know everything. Nobody knows everything. And an honest answer gives the other person more reliable data to work with.

Sometimes people are nosy. If someone asks you a question you would rather not answer, don't answer. Reply, "I prefer not to say." It is not unkind to avoid answering. It's just another kind of honesty. Sometimes people don't realize you have someone's privacy to protect. Or your own. Good people will understand.

Do you have trouble declining to answer nosy people? If so, practice different ways until you find one that is comfortable for you. Suggestions:

- "No, I can't say."
- "I'd rather not say."
- "Sorry, I can't say."
- "Can we talk about this later?"
- "I'd like to think about that. Can I get back to you later?"

Honest Communication

The best kind of communication is honest. Sometimes teenagers will tell people what they think the other person wants to hear, regardless of what their own ideas or feelings are. Being truthful avoids confusion and misunderstandings. It also helps you feel better about yourself, because it says that your ideas and feelings are worth respecting.

Some teenagers are afraid they will appear conceited if they show personal pride. You don't need to put yourself down if someone pays you a compliment. Simply say, "Thanks!" People like others who show confidence in themselves. You will not turn others off, so long as you recognize that the differing talents of others have equal value to yours.

Are you uncomfortable with compliments? If so, practice with your best friend, giving each other compliments until you both can readily smile and simply say, "Thank you."

It's okay to be honest about your negative feelings, as well. As was said earlier, admitting you are angry doesn't have to lead to a fistfight, name-calling, or backbiting. It often accomplishes the opposite. It releases your emotional pressure valve before it explodes into angry action.

If you speak up before your anger gets out of control, you can often talk out the problem in a normal or near-normal tone of voice. This way misunderstandings can be resolved before they go far.

What If I Can't Stand . . .?

You've probably have had at least one teacher by now that you can't stand. He or she just doesn't understand you. Or demands too much of you. Or you just don't like the way that person does things.

Unfortunately, your situation is not unusual. School is the workplace of young people. All people sooner or later have to work with persons they don't like or can't get along with well.

If you can't avoid working with that teacher, try hard to talk things out. Give it a good effort; if the relationship doesn't improve, you will at least know you tried.

If that doesn't help, try working around that person.

Listen to the lectures. Do the reading and other required work. Get the personal help you need from somewhere else—another student, another teacher, the librarian. Keep the one-on-one interaction with that person to a minimum.

Sometimes the climate is so bad between persons that a working relationship is impossible. If this is the case, talk to a counselor or the school principal. School authorities know these things happen. Unless your school situation is poor, they will try to make changes. They realize you can't learn well under this kind of stress.

You don't have to like all other people to have self-esteem. You don't have to like people to be nice to them and get along with them. There's a familiar saying, "You can't win them all." But you can usually get along with others if you are willing to work at it.

12.

Resolving Conflicts

When we strike out with a relationship problem, we can either walk away, or stay and try to work things out. If you can walk away and not hang on to your anger, that is probably the best way to go. But most people can't do that. If you are still mad hours later, it's best to confront your anger and talk out the problem with whomever offended you.

Talking out conflicts helps us to see where the other person is coming from. Suppose Bob had asked Dick, "Hey, why'd you do that?" Dick might have said, "Ah, gee, I'm sorry. I didn't mean any harm. Just got carried away, I guess."

Talking problems over makes us feel better faster. As was mentioned earlier, resentments, anger, or frustrations that are not resolved eat away at us. In the last chapter, Betty walked away from Mary. Had she stayed and talked, she would have learned the truth fast and both would have felt better about the situation and each other much sooner.

A Right Time and a Right Place

There is a right time and a wrong time to talk out problems. It's not a good idea to hit your dad with an argument right after he gets home from work. He's probably tired. Or to hit your mom when she's getting dinner ready. Give Dad fifteen minutes to relax. Ask Mom, "When can we talk?" And don't ask your parents for new gym shoes right after they get socked with a big car repair bill.

Sometimes things can't wait. If so, say so. We humans think other people know what's going on in our minds. They don't. We have to tell them. "This can't wait, Mom."

Try not to put other people on the spot. Mary rushed in the door one afternoon, saying, "Mom, can I go to the game? I have to leave in five minutes." She didn't give her mother much time to make the decision.

It's a good idea *not* to try to work things out when you are under pressure (have a big test to cram for) or when you feel sick. If you know you tend to be touchy at a certain time of the day (early morning, for instance), avoid arguments then, too. Everything looks blacker at these times, and it's harder to be nice.

There's a right and wrong place, too. Generally, it's not a good idea to talk family business in front of strangers or company. You don't want your parents to embarrass you in front of your friends. They feel the same way.

Talking Things Over Is Not Easy

Talking isn't as easy as it sounds. Communication is not an exact science. Even adults can't always say what they want to say. That's because an important part of us is our feelings, and it is hard to put feelings into words.

Feelings tell just as much as our thoughts do what it is we really want, but many times we human beings don't recognize those feelings. We know what our thoughts are, but that isn't enough. Sometimes the thoughts don't match the feelings. Then we don't know *what* we want.

For example, you may think you feel lonely and go to a movie with your best friend. After you get home, you may feel as bad as ever. It's obvious something else is bothering you.

When you confront others, they often return the anger. That is what makes this kind of communication so hard. We don't want to say anything for fear we'll lose a friendship or hurt the other person's feelings. So we bury *our* feelings, which is just as bad because our feelings are important, too, and buried anger never goes away.

You can minimize the unpleasantness of confronting by following a simple formula: listen to the other side, state your case clearly without finding fault, share your feelings, show that you care, and fight fair.

- *Listen to the other side* of the argument. Hear with an open mind. Try to see the situation through the other person's eyes. He or she *may* be right. (You can admit this, even if *you* don't agree. What's wrong for you might be right for her or him.)

- If, after hearing the other person, you are still

angry, *state your case clearly.* Tell how *you* see the situation. Be as direct as you can be. Don't beat around the bush. Attack the *problem*, not the *person.* Your goal is to restore a damaged relationship. It does more harm than good to tear down the other person in the process.

Restate your case if the other person is not hearing you accurately: "I'm not making myself clear. . . ." Then use other words to explain your thoughts.

- *Share your feelings.* Tell how the incident made you feel. Use words like tacky, crummy, frustrated, worthless, disgusted, sad, scared, heartbroken, disappointed, irritated, or angry. Perhaps, "I was down in the dumps all day about this."

- *Show that you care* about the other person. Tell mom how unhappy you are about the way things are since the argument. Mention how much you want to work things out with your locker partner so that you can get back to being friends again.

Caring also involves giving the other person time and space—whatever he or she needs to work out the problem. We don't all bring the same intensity to a situation. We come to terms with it at different rates of time. True caring does not crowd the other person.

Suppose Mary had been late because she didn't watch the time. She felt guilty, so she didn't dare tell Betty. She might need time to come to terms with that. If Mary doesn't want to talk things out, Betty could say, "Whenever you are ready. . . ."

- *Fight fair.* Be aboveboard in your dealings with the other person. Don't go behind his or her back and tell false tales or build enemy support.

If you have contributed to the problem by baiting the other person, admit it. Were you just itching for a fight? If you caused the problem, make it up to that person as best you can. If you don't see where you've gone wrong, try to find out why your behavior caused the other person trouble.

It's good to apologize even if you haven't done anything wrong. It benefits your self-esteem. Asking forgiveness doesn't necessarily mean that you intentionally set out to hurt someone. Sometimes trouble just happens.

Suppose your elbow happens to be in the way when your friend leans over to set his books on the table, causing him to spill them all over the floor. Did you do something wrong? Of course not. "I'm sorry" in this kind of situation is a way of saying "I feel sad because I caused you trouble, even if I didn't do anything wrong."

When you apologize, don't bend over backwards about it. "Oh, I'm *so* sorry. I know you'll *never* forgive me. . . ." Just apologize and then go on. A simple "I'm sorry" looks and feels better than carrying on.

If other people have wronged you, it is kind as well as a boost to your self-esteem to let them off the hook gracefully. Don't hold out, or ask for penance. Just accept their apology and then forget about it. You'll like yourself better, and so will they.

Ways of Settling Things

Many times we have to give and take to settle disputes. There are several ways to do this.

The most familiar is called *compromise*. This means that both parties give a bit until they reach dead center. Both sacrifice something, but neither gives up everything.

You and a friend both want to go out. You have your heart set on a movie. Your friend is dying to go bowling. Instead you end up going to the teen hangout. Neither of you really wanted to go there, but you couldn't agree on anything else.

Another method of settling things is to *find a middle ground* that both of you like. You want to wear jeans. Your friend wants to wear slacks. But both of you are comfortable and feel well-dressed in corduroys.

Middle ground is better than compromise because neither of you is sacrificing anything. It's harder to come by, however, because you can't always find a middle ground.

Sometimes you can *trade off*. "If you'll go with me to the movies tonight, I'll go bowling with you next week."

The hardest way of all is to *give in*. We all have to give in from time to time. It isn't always necessary or desirable. Much depends upon the situation and especially how deeply you and the other person feel about things.

Is this movie something you've been waiting to see for months? Tell your friend, "We can go bowling anytime, but this movie's only going to be in town this week. . . ." If the other person wants to go bowling to watch the state tournament and the movie was just another good science fiction treat, you would be the logical one to give in.

To help you practice conflict resolution skills, imagine the following situation:

You just saw a friend going to a movie with someone else. You are angry because this person had told you he/she had too much homework to go out with you.

- State your case: "Sam, I saw you at the movie with Joe."
- Listen. (Is there possibly a good reason?)
- Explain your feelings. "I feel angry, letdown, deceived. . . ."
- Tell how much you care. "I want to be your friend and be able to trust you."
- Admit any misunderstandings or wrongs on your part. "Did I say I was going to be busy? Oh, I forgot!"
- Forgive. "Okay, so you goofed this time and left me out. I can see that you feel bad. It's okay. We can still be friends."

13.

Building Friendships

The biblical friends, David and Jonathan, were such good buddies they would have given their lives for each other. Professional football players Gayle Sayers and Brian Piccolo of the Chicago Bears had the same kind of friendship, as could be seen in the television movie, "Brian's Song." Piccolo helped Sayers get back in shape after a knee injury, even though it meant he might lose his chance to play in the games. Sayers supported Piccolo and his family when Piccolo's bout with cancer came.

* * *

You have been making friends ever since you learned that playing with other toddlers in the neighborhood could be more fun than playing alone. When you started school, you began spending lots of time with people your own age.

As you grow up and away from your parents and family, friends will fill your need for outside support and broaden your horizons. Even those teens who are close to their parents need someone else's ideas to test theirs against. Your friends may soon play as important a role in your life as your parents.

The friendships we make are vitally important. Good ones sometimes last a lifetime.

Making Friends

Many people, teenagers included, find it hard to make new friends. It's difficult for most people to walk up and talk to a stranger. We are ill at ease breaking the ice.

There are a couple of ways to overcome this shyness. One is to remind yourself that the other person is probably just as uneasy as you are. You can help both of you by searching for something you have in common. What classes is this person taking? Is he or she in band? On an athletic team? Where does this person live? Does he or she like school?

If you don't want to make the first move, ask a mutual friend to introduce you. Or, if you see a circle of acquaintances talking with someone new, walk up and start talking to the persons you know. Then after a few minutes, stick out your hand and say, "Hi, I don't think I've met you. My name is ———."

If you find you don't have anything in common, ask questions about some subject in which that person has expressed an interest. People love to talk about the things that turn them on. You will learn something new, and you might even pick up the interest yourself. This is the way friendships broaden our horizons.

Your response to the person (listening and giving visual and verbal approval) is as important as the questions you ask or what you say. It shows your interest in that person is genuine.

You may want to share *your* interests, too, but don't overdo. Watch for signs of lagging interest. If you see the other person's eyes moving away, change the subject so you don't become a bore.

If the conversation lags from time to time, that's okay. You don't have to fill every minute with conversation. Both you and the other person need time to think of what to say next.

If too much time goes by and the conversation is not going, excuse yourself and move on. Not every encounter is going to turn into a workable friendship. "See you later" is an acceptable sign-off.

With some people you will hit it off right away. You will find much in common or develop an immediate liking. In these situations, it's okay to let that person know you would like to continue the relationship. "Hey, call me sometime."

If the feeling is shared, you'll get a good response. "Yeah, I will."

If not, you are not obligating that person to anything. "We'll see. . . ." Don't push yourself on others. If the friendship was meant to fly, it will.

In order to make friends, one has to be a good friend. This means accepting other people as they are—appearance, personality, and attitudes—complete with their faults. Friends overlook each other's faults often, confronting only when it's necessary to settle a serious problem quickly.

Choosing Good Friends

The kinds of friends you choose will have a lot to do with how well you sail through your teenage years. The right kinds of friends reinforce our good habits and moral values. They confirm our good feelings about ourselves. Poor friends can cause us all kinds of grief.

How do you know whether a friend is a *good* friend or a *poor* one? Look for good character traits:

- Is this person honest? *Truthfulness* is precious. One never knows what to believe from persons who lie, even if they only do so occasionally. You can't be completely comfortable with them.

- Another quality to look for is *kindness*. There are gentle, caring people in this world, and there are mean-spirited persons who don't care who they hurt as long as they get what they want. A kind person treats others well, friend or not. It's nice to know you will get such treatment if you end up disagreeing with your friend from time to time.

- *Gentleness* is another good quality. It is *not* a feminine trait, as some think. It takes a great deal of mental strength and courage to resist violence as did Jesus, Martin Luther King, Jr., and Mohandas Gandhi. Toughness (the macho kind) can be just a cover for weakness. Men with gentle strength don't need to advertise their power.

- *Loyalty* is another important characteristic you will want your friends to have. This doesn't mean that they shouldn't have other friends. It just means that they will support you when someone else attacks your reputation.

The loyal friend doesn't swing from one group of friends to another, just to be *in*. This person values friendships more than being part of a certain crowd.

- *Dependability* is important, too, if you don't want your friends to waste your time or let you down. It's nice to know that a friend will be there if he says he will. Or that if he can't, he will call and let you know.

- Another important character quality, one that is undervalued in our part of the world, is *obedience.* This means a cooperative spirit and respect for assigned authority. Such a friend follows rules, unless there is a vitally important reason not to.

The earlier character qualities affected how a friend gets along with you. This one helps determine how well you will get along in the world.

Why Is Obedience Important?

We are all part of a bigger picture—the communities in which we live. They include our family, school, church, city or county, state, and country. We have as much responsibility to these communities as we do to ourselves.

People living together in community need guidelines to maintain dependable patterns of living. Order disappears when laws are not followed. Chaos results.

Our highest call is to obey God and his commandments. Doing that also means submitting to civil laws and school and house rules. People have to know what to expect of others if they are to live in harmony.

If your friends cooperate with authority persons at home, in school, and in your community, then you probably will, too. Why? Because, whether you intend to or not, you tend to become like your friends.

All of us are constantly changing our ideas about things. As we learn something new, we begin to see that item or situation a bit differently. In the process our thinking can get distorted. You won't always recognize immediately that a certain new idea making the rounds in your crowd doesn't work well.

The friend who urges you to obey existing laws and listen to the voice of experience can save you much grief and embarrassment. Some day you may have to buck the crowd. It isn't easy. It takes courage. This kind of friend can be an invaluable ally in such a situation.

I Want to Be "In"

Most high schools have one or more *in-groups*, cliques which control the social climate. Everybody wants to belong. It feels good to be accepted by your peers. But not everybody gets in.

It appears on the surface that your self-esteem rides on your being in an in-group. That is not the case. Whether you join one or not, your self-esteem is based on *your* thinking and feelings about yourself, not somebody else's. Just as nobody else can build your self-esteem for you, nobody else can take it away or determine it for you.

But that fact does not take away the pressure of living in a socially conscious society. What do you do if you want to be *in*, but can't make it?

It hurts to feel rejected. You're faced with a difficult problem, but not necessarily a disastrous one. There will be a lot of other students in the same predicament. You can build your circle of friends around them.

It helps to realize that any group that discriminates without good reason (bad moral habits or drug use) is not a caring, sensitive group. They have a problem—the need to be exclusive. The relationships such a group builds are apt to be unhealthy ones. Because they are insensitive, they may let each other down frequently. You can have something better—open, caring relationships with your companions.

It may be hard for you to get in because you have a bad reputation or have some habit that irritates people a lot. If so, the answer is to correct your bad habit or rebuild your reputation. Treat people well, change what is poor, and give yourself time. If you have a bad standing that is undeserved, ask friends who know the truth to spread the word in the right places.

Suppose you are part of the *in-group*, and like being there, even though it discriminates unfairly. You need to be aware of the consequences. Do you feel guilty? How are the group members treating each other? Are you resented by those who don't make it? Can you, by being part of the group, help to open it up to others and thus be a good influence? If not, is it worth it?

14.

My Sexual Self

It took Matthew several days to get up the courage to ask Melissa for a date to the school prom. Dad said he could have the car, if he was careful and bought his own gas. He rented a tux. Melissa was his first choice as a date, and he was in heaven when she said yes.

Melissa wanted to go badly, and was so hoping Matthew would ask her. When Matthew finally did, she was in ecstasy. She spent hours shopping for a gown. On the big day, she got a sophisticated cut and bouffant hairstyle at her mom's favorite salon. It took her two hours to get dressed.

When Matt picked her up, he brought an orchid corsage. Melissa opened it. "Oh . . ." she said, disappointed. It was withered and brown. Matt had put it in the freezer to keep it fresh, but it froze. Melissa said that was okay, but Matt still felt bad.

As they walked out to the car, gusts of wind

swirled about the car, whipping Melissa's hairdo. When she got to the prom she went to the ladies' room to repair the damage. Friends helped her, but her hair still didn't look right. She started to cry.

When she came out, she told Matt she wanted to go home.

"You look fine," he said.

"You're just being nice," Melissa shot back angrily.

"Let's go for a drive."

"I don't *want* to go for a drive. I want to go home."

They were shouting. People started to stare at them, so Melissa said, "Okay." Matt drove her around town for half an hour, hoping that she would calm down and change her mind. Instead, he ran out of gas. He walked to the nearest gas station and back, but spilled gasoline on his tux as he filled the tank.

They both went home, dejected.

* * *

First dates don't usually end as disastrously as Matt and Melissa's did, but the ingredients are there. As their sexuality begins to mature, teens become nervous around members of the opposite sex. Their social situation is undergoing rapid and marked change. It takes time to learn new ways. Anxious moments and embarrassing incidents are bound to happen.

What Is Sexuality?

From the day you were born you were treated in a special way because of your sex. From the same-sex parent a child learns certain roles (ways of living and relating to others). Daughters are their father's "sweethearts." Sons are their mother's "pals."

Parents tend to treat a child of the opposite sex in a fairly relaxed manner, since they don't set the example for that child. They tend to be more demanding with a child of their own sex because they have to establish the pattern for that child's behavior. It's a big responsibility.

As adolescence approaches and their reproductive organs mature, teens become more aware of the differences between the sexes. They find themselves with an attraction to the opposite sex that was not there before. This is all part of God's beautiful plan to bring men and women together for close, warm friendship and to create new family units and assure the continuation of human life.

Sexuality involves not only the body, but also emotional responses. Men in our culture have been trained to conceal emotion. Crying is supposedly a sign of weakness. Hugging and kissing are thought to be "womanly" traits, not to be openly displayed.

Fortunately these foolish and unhealthy notions are changing. Men are just as capable of love and compassion as women are. They too need the affection and warmth that come from touching experiences (the arm around the shoulder, the hand on the arm). Men as well as women need to release their negative emotions in healing ways. It's okay to cry if your dog dies or your parents are getting a divorce. Better that than punching out a brick wall or crashing your bike.

Women have been trained by past societies to show weakness in difficult situations. Luckily this is also changing. Girls need and ought not feel ashamed to take a strong stand with gossipers who threaten their reputations or friends who "borrow" (without asking) their sweaters from their lockers.

Feeling at Ease with the Opposite Sex

As sexuality develops, teenagers normally have trouble feeling comfortable around members of the opposite sex. They fear they may say or do the wrong thing and embarrass themselves.

It helps to realize that all teenagers go through this. Boys and girls alike find themselves tongue-tied when they spot someone they would like to meet and get to know. Parties help. So does attendance at mixed events at school, church, or in the community. The more teens associate in mixed groups, the more at ease they become.

What should you do if you think you flubbed an attempt to get acquainted with a member of the opposite sex? Strive for poise. For some, that means walking quietly away. For others, it means holding your head up, grinning, shrugging your shoulders, and going on as if nothing happened. Some will be able to clear away the discomfort by laughing about it.

If you choose to cope by joking and laughing at yourself, don't put yourself down. Your friends don't want you to feel like a loser, only a normal person for whom something didn't work out.

Dating

Most teenagers look forward to the time they can begin dating members of the opposite sex. It's glamorous. Books, movies, and songs are filled with stories of tender, romantic love affairs. Who doesn't want to be loved like that?

Life is not always like the movies, however. In the movies the teenage heroine always looks like she just stepped out of the beauty shop. She did. Real life experience is more like that of Matt and Melissa. Guys fall flat on their faces in front of their desired heartthrob. Girls spill taco sauce on their blouses. In real life it takes time to be able to cope with the unexpected and to visit comfortably with the opposite sex.

Dating carries with it a responsibility, one taken too lightly by society today. You get a crush on someone. You manage to get acquainted and finally to date. Wow! It's a dream come true. You want to show your affection with a good-night kiss. And hug. Or, better yet, lots of them. After several dates, *necking* may become an enjoyable and delightful part of your relationship.

Mild expressions of affection are okay, if the persons involved are in control of their emotions. But caressing someone of the opposite sex builds up emotional energies that are hard to handle. Too much hugging and kissing can lead to *petting* (the caressing of other body parts), which can in turn lead to full sexual arousal.

The sex drive is a powerful force. It has a beautiful purpose and value in the expression of love and the creation of new life. But the sex act can be selfish. It needs restraint, control, and a lifetime commitment in order to become a good vehicle for expressing unselfish love.

Love is so glamorized by society today and self-control so minimized that young people stumble into shallow, heavily physical relationships before they are emotionally ready. Girls are getting pregnant and boys becoming fathers long before they want the responsibility of settling down with one person and raising a family.

When persons lose control of their sexual appetites, they are left with strong feelings of guilt and fear. The emotionally wrenching problems of breakups caused by a lack of commitment and maturity, unwanted pregnancy, venereal disease, and AIDS are a hefty price to pay. Even those who use birth control devices are not completely safe, nor are they free of guilt and fear.

About Self-control

Self-control is not only possible, it is essential to your sense of well-being. It is also on the way back as a social trend, according to a noted health education expert. Ann Landers also recommends it. And so does the Bible.

Self-control is not difficult to come by if you take your time learning how to handle yourself gracefully around the opposite sex. Contrary to what you hear in the locker room, sex without love and the commitment of marriage is not really all that much fun. It takes time to develop skill in communicating and relating.

Suggested guidelines: Acquire good social skills before you start dating. When you do date, save the kissing and hugging for that *someone special.* (Even if the guy is footing the bill, that does not entitle him nor is the girl obligated to "pay" for the evening with kisses or other sexual favors.) And, don't go past the necking stage.

Some will say, "But we just had to 'have' each other because we fell in love. . . ." That's not love talking, but a lack of self-control.

It is possible for the seeds of a mature, lasting

love to develop during your teenage years. But it is also hard to tell whether you're in love with the other person, on a passionate *high*, or just in love with *being in love*. Many a teenager has mistaken the last two for the real thing and ended up with a bitter, broken relationship. Or a marriage that turned sour within a few years. Real love can wait, and does.

Sexual Preferences

Having a distinct sexuality is important to good emotional health. There is a functional place in society for the masculinity of men, just as there is a place for the femininity of women. The two work together for joyful relationships and the creation, care, and nurturing of new life.

Some people are oriented differently in their sexuality. Transvestites (cross-dressers), homosexuals, and lesbians experience urges uncommon for males and females, as God created them. Homosexuals and lesbians prefer sexual intercourse with persons of their own sex. Same-sex preferences by a small segment of society have been in existence since the earliest recorded times. Society has not yet found the causes of homosexuality. Much study has been done in recent years. A few groups are reporting success in treating those who desire a heterosexual or opposite-sex orientation.

One can have such feelings and still decide not to act on them. Self-control is possible. Unnatural sexual relations are not generally accepted by society—causing ostracism. The Bible speaks against them, too, though theologians differ in interpreting why.

There has been a movement by homosexuals and

lesbians for acceptance of their lifestyle. Now with the AIDS epidemic, more people recognize hazards for those having sexual relations outside normal heterosexual marriage.

If you are now or someday find yourself having lesbian or homosexual responses, it is very important for your self-esteem that you get professional help to deal with the stress it causes. Good counseling by properly trained persons can help you build your life in a constructive manner.

The appropriate response for those who find themselves in the company of a homosexual or lesbian person is one of courtesy, and respect. All persons are made in the image of God.

Flaunting Your Sexuality

Sometimes men and women dress to accentuate their sexuality with, for example, tight pants. Low-cut blouses or dresses which reveal a woman's cleavage call attention to her sexual features. Some people similarly like to talk a lot about the sex act and sexual organs and to walk in ways that advertise their sexiness.

This kind of dress, behavior, and speech have nothing to do with a person's true sexuality or lack of it. People who have a healthy sexuality don't need to promote it. The appropriate attitude of the sexually healthy person is one of modesty and respect for the privacy due one's own and others' private body parts.

Am I in Love?

Ahead of you lie some of the most interesting, exciting years of your life. Some of you will choose chastity and dedication to a vocation with God or a demanding career. Most of you will fall in love and marry as part of your service to God. Some will choose their life partner before they leave their teens, though most wait till later.

How do you know if you are in love? A true *in-love* relationship is one that offers deep friendship as well as companionship—shared interests and activities. It can stand the test of time, separation, distance (if you should move apart), and other friendships.

People fall in love when they are ready to make a commitment. Your self-esteem will be greater and that commitment stronger if you acquire some independent living skills and experiences before making any relationship a permanent one.

15.

Handling the Hard Times

Your mom and dad just walked in, sat down with you, and told you they are getting a divorce. Your world suddenly collapses. You saw some symptoms of trouble, but you never expected things would go this far.

How could this be happening? You love them both. You want them together. Most of all, you want *all* of you, including your brothers and sisters, to be together. You've seen in the lives of friends how painful it is to be divided between parents. You would do *anything* to keep your folks together. But you can't.

Life Has Ups and Downs

Life has a rhythm—good days and poor ones, good years and bad ones. It would be nice if life were perfect, or even nearly so, but it isn't. Sooner or later everybody has bumps in the road.

They may come from unfortunate circumstances, like when you get the flu or when a late frost destroys a farmer's fruit crop. Sometimes we bring them on ourselves. As when you didn't study for a course and flunked it. Sometimes they come from other people's choices that affect you. As when your best friend moved away because his dad got promoted to sales manager. (You thought you would be friends for life. You hadn't figured that families in certain types of businesses move often.)

Self-esteem is hard to keep when troubles come. You can't feel good about yourself when you see that F on your report card. Or when you walk into the school cafeteria and there's a hole in your stomach because that familiar face isn't there to eat lunch with.

There are things you can think and do to make hard times a bit easier.

Handling Troubles with Grace

One thing is to remember that you probably don't look as bad as you feel. In coping with small problems and disappointments, most people continue their habits of personal care and living. It's only the inner core that gets a bit out of joint.

Leaning on your support system helps. Your best friend will understand if you goofed off in a course; he or she is human, too. But don't use your support system to excuse negligence. You must accept your own fair share of responsibility for the upset if you are to have inner peace.

It helps, too, to see troubles as stepping stones. Adversity can be a teacher. Using mistakes and troubles as growing experiences is more likely to improve your self-esteem.

Losses

Just as good relationships are our greatest source of joy in living, so also the loss of someone or something dear to us causes us the greatest pain. Losing a boyfriend or girlfriend hurts. If death has taken a beloved grandparent, a schoolmate, or a pet, you know how heavy grief can be.

There are several kinds of losses, all of which cause anguish. Moving to another community means the loss of a familiar home, school, your favorite stores and hangouts, and friends. Loss of health occasionally strikes teenagers, as does loss of a limb or other body part through accident or illness. Divorce is also a major loss—not only the tearing apart of the family unit but also the change of lifestyle from what you had when you were all together.

Losses are difficult for people of any age to cope with. They are also quite common, with so many families moving and today's high divorce rate. Unlike some kinds of troubles, you can't avoid them, but there are several things you can do to make them more bearable.

Handling Losses

• First and most important, *accept what you cannot change.* You are going to aggravate the situation if you try to fight a battle you cannot win. You cannot make your parent's marriage work. If you ignore your diabetes, you could be in trouble.

Accept the loss as a new but normal part of your existence. Accepting a painful loss does not mean that you are helpless to do anything about it. You don't need to let the loss wipe you out.

• Second, *meet the problem head-on.* Like waves

in the face, adversity tends to startle us. Prepare for it by realizing there will be "those kinds of days and years." We cause ourselves a lot of grief by expecting only sunny days from God and perfection from ourselves, our parents, our families and friends, and life.

Difficult times are a part of life. Everybody faces the death of someone dear sooner or later. We don't like it. We don't want it. We certainly don't ask for it. So we try to pretend it isn't happening. Or we run. That delays the healing.

- *Ask God for help.* There are times in the lives of everybody when they cannot handle their pain alone. It is a proven fact that those who look beyond themselves in faith tap a source of power and strength that helps them through.

God wants us to bring our problems to him. He asks us to. You need not carry your burden alone. Ask God to get you through the day, the hour, or even the minute, if your pain is that great and pressing. Mentally turn your hurt over to him. "Give me strength and wisdom, God. I can't handle this by myself." He brings a peacefulness in the midst of pain that only those who've been there can understand.

- *Expect to grieve for your loss,* no matter what kind it is. You can miss good health as much as a dearly loved grandpa, if not more. You can miss "the way things used to be" before the divorce, even if there were problems then. You can miss a tooth, especially a front one, that is knocked out in an accident.

Grieving of any kind comes in five stages: *denial* (this isn't happening), *anger* (this shouldn't be happening), *bargaining* (if you will undo this, Lord,

I'll do . . . for you), *dawning awareness* (it really is happening), and *acceptance* (it's okay; I will survive). Grief counselors tell us you need to proceed through all of these emotional stages to heal properly and get on with your life.

- *Give yourself plenty of time.* It takes months or years to adjust; one expert suggests three years for deep losses. It speeds the process if you set your mind to working through the feelings. You won't get there by avoiding them—they just go underground and erupt later.

- *Be kind to yourself,* and to others. You may be miserable, but it won't help you or your family if you get crabby because you're in a down mood on a certain day. Silence is okay. Better yet, change the scene. Go someplace, or do something different.

- You need to *talk out your loss,* however. When you do, try not to feel sorry for yourself. It'll only make you feel worse. Feel sorry about the situation, or the condition you have to live with, remembering that many others have been there, too. Unfortunately, trouble is universal.

Cherish the good times you had before it happened. It helps to remember them and to realize that they are treasures you need not surrender.

- It's okay to *own up to the accompanying feelings*—disappointment, frustration, resentment, and other negative feelings: Boy, it really threw me bad when Brian moved. I've felt like crying for weeks! . . . I'm so sad without my cocker, Spotty. She just meant *everything* to me!. . . I *hate* what's happening to me! How will I *ever* be able to live a normal life on a diabetic diet?

It helps you to heal when you admit you have these feelings. Bad feelings don't necessarily lead to bad behaviors. Nor are they a source for embarrassment. You are not unusual. Many others have had to face losses. Those who have will understand your reactions. Those who haven't will, someday, when they have losses to face.

- *Pamper yourself* a bit. You especially need to feel good about yourself during times of deep loss. So if you like strawberry shakes, indulge for awhile. Buy something new to wear. Or a new record. Or take a trip to visit a friend or favorite relative.

- *Get back in the mainstream of living* as fast as you can. In other words, keep busy. Find a hobby. Make new friends, or go visit the old. Take extra classes. Join a club. It's amazing how fast things will seem normal again once you start acting like they are.

- *Remember that hard times don't last.* A common saying goes, "This, too, shall pass." Life does go on. Things do get better. It's part of the rhythm of life that, after the long dark night, the sun does rise again. People adjust, even to radical change, sooner or later.

- *Positive thinking is a benefit.* You have two choices—to nurse your deep hurt or to make the best of things. Feeling sorry for yourself makes you feel worse. The determination to *hang tough* by waiting it out and doing what you can to rise above the problem will make you feel better faster.

- It also helps to *make a plan of action.* If there is something you can do about your problem, plan what to do and how you will go about it. If your family is moving to another state, perhaps you could return to spend the summer with your best friend.

Even if the situation is out of your control, you

can plan different ways of coping with it. You can't visit each other? Until you've both had a chance to build other close friendships, perhaps you and your friend can agree to write every other day for a time and call each other on the phone occasionally.

Getting started on your plan puts you somewhat in control of your life again. You are no longer a helpless victim. This in itself will raise your spirits.

- Don't fail to *look for support* from other family members and your friends. Don't try to handle grief alone. Good relationships involve give and take. This year (or today) it's your turn to lean on somebody else. Next year (or tomorrow) someone may need to turn to you for help. Life's greatest opportunities for showing love come from helping one another in times of serious trouble.

I Don't Like Life Anymore

Problems depress us. So does too much stress. Or pain. Losses also can cause a temporary but severe physical illness called *clinical depression*. Chemical changes in our bodies can also affect or bring on this sickness.

When it strikes, people lose their zest for living. They have headaches, can't sleep at night, lose their appetite, or have a sour stomach. They may be tired all the time and feel hopeless about rising above their situation. In severe cases, they can become suicidal.

Everybody gets the blues now and then. If you are caught up in a depressed mood for a short period of time, the same suggestions that work for losses will help you bounce back. If, however, you experience most or all of the above symptoms for a prolonged period of time (two to four weeks or more), or if they keep recurring, you need medical assistance. Appropriate medicines can shorten the time and lessen the severity of clinical depression.

Some people hesitate to go for help, thinking they should be able to pull themselves together. But severe depression devastates the human spirit. It is a major medical problem. It can incapacitate people's ability to help themselves. And it can kill. The smart thing to do is to get professional help, since relief is readily available.

What If My Home Life Is Poor?

Some teenagers have a permanently difficult home life. Their parents are alcoholic or abusive, or they have a permanently disabled brother who demands everybody's time and attention. A live-in grandmother constantly criticizes them, or a mentally retarded sister is always hanging around, pestering.

In these kinds of situations, you need to learn how to cope. You probably have needs of your own that are being overlooked. If you can't handle things alone or with your parents' help, get outside help through counseling.

Your school counselor might be able to help. If not, there are many good counseling agencies in most larger communities today. Your pastor or priest or a teacher will gladly counsel with you or make sure you find a suitable counselor.

The counselor's job is to help you find options you probably had not realized were available to you to make progress in solving your problem. If there is no way to work out the situation, the counselor may be able to arrange respite—a vacation away from the problem for awhile. Often such a break makes bearable what we thought was unbearable.

16.

Looking Ahead

Your teen years are marvelously exciting years. Adventure and discovery lie ahead. In the next few years you will be finding yourself, solidifying your interests, and opening yourself to a bigger world. You will be learning to drive, getting your first full-time job, going out on your own, and maybe even finding a lifetime marriage partner.

These are also dangerous years. One careless or reckless night can bring an unwanted pregnancy, manslaughter by drunk driving, crippling injury, or similar wrenching problems. It's hard to hang onto your self-esteem if such a thing happens. Even if you don't run into serious trouble, it's hard to find self-esteem in a society that says that looks, brains, power, and money matter above everything else.

This book has tried to show you a more effective and satisfying route. If it has proved helpful to you, reread it occasionally. If the personal inventory you filled out makes you feel good about yourself, look it over often, particularly if you're feeling a little down on yourself. But most of all, keep giving yourself those good messages that steer you on a sound path for good and godly living.

Remember every day that you are God's beloved child. You are precious. You are unique. You are important to your Lord and to your family. And you are needed by them.

Do your best with what God has given you. Get your advice from reliable sources. Take good care of yourself, on the inside as well as the outside. Find what you are good at, and do it. Hold on to your values. Treasure your relationships. Build solid friendships. Use your sexuality wisely, as God intended. And take God with you across the mountains as well as through the valleys of life.

When Will I Have It Made?

Will you have it made by the end of your teens? No. But you will be starting to pull it all together—what you are, how life is, and what you want to do with what you are.

You will never *arrive*, because we are imperfect human beings. We are always in the process of becoming.

Fortunately, your self-esteem does not depend on making the goals you set for yourself. It comes from appreciating who and what you are as you walk the road of life—all the way along that road. You can have it today, if you will see yourself as God sees you.

Be Open to God

The most important thing you can do for yourself as you walk that road is to open yourself to God's guidance and direction. To see yourself as his beloved creation and the natural world as his masterpiece is a treasure only God-related people know. To do God's thing instead of your own is to open the door to a far more satisfying, loving existence than many people ever experience in a whole lifetime.

A few months ago, I noticed that during conversations with my best friend I was frequently turning him off. I asked God to show me why. Not long afterward, I began listening to myself. I heard a lot of faultfinding. I asked God to close my mouth whenever I felt like criticizing. I worked at it, too. I'm quieter now. I like myself a lot better. I noticed that my best friend seems more comfortable around me. He's sharing more of his ideas with me.

God can help you, too, if you let him. He wants to. He will provide ideas, direction, strength, and loving support whenever we need them. Whenever we ask. Often through others who know God.

Best of all, God never makes a mistake. Whatever problem we turn over to him, even if things look like they are turning out all wrong, will become right for us and will eventually bring his promised goodness into our lives.

God can do far more to make us happy, and happy with ourselves, than we can by following our own route. Why not let him?

Looking at Me

Physical characteristics. A list of my nice features: (eyes, ears, nose, mouth, shape of face, hair, shape of body, nice smile, good coloring, good proportions, freckles, dimples, good legs, graceful hands, or whatever): _____
_____
_____

Loving me _____

Interests. What I like to do in my spare time: sports, music, art, drama, reading, writing, mechanics, sewing, cooking, handcrafts, gardening or farming, animal care, photography, horseback riding, computers, or _____ .
List the *kind* of pastime (swimming, singing, etc.): _____
_____
_____

Loving me _____

Skills, talents (things I do well or am learning to be good at). Select from interests: _____
_____
_____
_____

Loving me _____

Personality traits. What I am most often: Perceptive, soft-spoken, easygoing, a conformer, observant, dreamer, lively, popular, speak up easily, hardworking, a doer, sociable, unorganized, tough, generous, cheerful, humorous, gentle, thrifty, sensitive, thoughtful, idealistic, artistic, a leader, quiet, or _____

Loving me _____

Character traits. Those which describe me: Honest, obedient, reverent, do not curse, loyal, loving, kind, friendly, brave, courteous, patient, helpful, dependable, responsible, conscientious, no dirty stories, speak well of other people, keep promises, fair, or _____

Loving me _____

Hopes, dreams, and goals. My dreams for the future are
_____
_____
_____

Loving me _____

My Listeners

Names *Phone numbers*

The Author

Margaret Houk's fondness for young people motivated her into counseling at summer camps, in college dorms, as a foster parent, with girl and boy scouts, and in church teaching settings. Her favorite involvement is with those eleven to fifteen years of age. She says, "This is such a critical period. Vulnerable but still pliable, early teens are at the most difficult, most dangerous, and most impressionable stage of their lives."

Houk's deep personal need felt in the ashes of a burnout years ago led her into a closer relationship with God and on an ardent quest for improved emotional health. She found that self-esteem is God's will and vital to loving unselfishly. She speaks out with devout faith, realism, and informed knowledge—sharing the insights she has received about God, his will, life, relationships, and love.

She has a B.S. degree in home economics from Valparaiso University with minors in social sciences, education, and English. A Bethel Bible Series teacher, she began writing in 1971 and is now widely published in many religious and general-interest magazines. She has won several writing awards.

Born and raised in Grand Rapids, Michigan, she presently lives in Appleton, Wisconsin, with her husband, John Peter. She is active in Prince of Peace Lutheran Church and in many ecumenical, social, and charitable efforts in her community. Four adult children and eight grandchildren enrich her life. For fun she sings, reads, gardens, does needlework, cross-country skis, and travels.